*"The best single organizational document ever written.
Ford workers read this book aloud to their families.*
The Flivver King *helped found our union."*

WALTER REUTHER


"The Flivver King *made an enormous contribution
to the ultimate success
of the drive to unionize Ford."*

VICTOR REUTHER

# THE
# FLIVVER KING

"*A classic novel from the UAW's early days.*"
—Mike Matejka, *UAW Solidarity*

"*A magnificent tale, told softly but pungently.*"
—Sidney Lens, *The Progressive*

"*Sinclair outlasted most of the 1930s proletarian novelists;
he etched some of his most unforgettable portraits
at the end of his long career.* The Flivver King,
*published thirty years after he became world-famous
for* The Jungle, *may be his most memorable work.*"
—*Village Voice*

"*In 1933 I worked for the Briggs Manufacturing Co.,
a builder of Ford bodies. I worked under Ford conditions
and for Ford wages. I became a leader in a strike,
and in 1937 I became a volunteer UAW organizer of Ford workers.
I saw* The Flivver King *when it was first published in 1937
and am glad to give the new Kerr edition my full endorsement.
I want a hundred copies to sell to UAW members.*"
—John Anderson

"*An ideal novel to hand someone who needs to be told
how capitalism works and why we need unions.*"
—Fred Thompson, *Industrial Worker*

Upton Sinclair

# THE
# FLIVVER KING
## A Story of Ford-America

# UPTON SINCLAIR

Introduction by Steve Meyer

CHARLES H. KERR  LABOR CLASSICS

## Charles H. Kerr Publishing Company
*Established 1886*
Chicago
1999

New ISBN 978-0-88286-357-3
Old system 0-88286-357-6


Earlier ISBN 0-88286-054-2

**CHARLES H. KERR PUBLISHING COMPANY**
1726 West Jarvis Avenue, Chicago, IL 60626
www.charleshkerr.net

# Introduction

Against the backdrop of the current economic malaise throughout the American industrial Midwest, the republication of Upton Sinclair's *The Flivver King* offers a fascinating glimpse at history: a vivid social and economic picture of the making of the auto-industrial age in the first decades of this century. Much like contemporary television docu-drama, this powerful story of "Ford-America" is a dramatic blend of fact and fiction. In this short novel, Sinclair presents a realistic account of the social origins and consequences of the "Second Industrial Revolution"—the rise of automotive mass production.

Upton Sinclair (1878-1968) was a master in the use of the novel to convey a deep sense of the social realities of modern industrial America. He grew up during the rise of an aggressive industrial capitalism in the United States. Educated at New York City College and Columbia, he joined the Socialist Party in 1902 and began his lifelong efforts to rectify the evils and abuses of an insensitive industrial system. In the Progressive Era, he was a writer in the "muckraking" tradition, exposing the whole gamut of social and industrial ills. His most famous work, *The Jungle* (1906), documented the conditions of immigrant workers in Chicago's meatpacking industry; it also demonstrated Sinclair's remarkable ability to integrate a mass of factual data into fictional form. In numerous less well-known novels, he took on the dominant institutions and attitudes of his times—religion in *The Profits of Religion* (1918), war in *Jimmy Higgins* (1919), the press in *The Brass Check* (1919), education in *The Goose Step* (1923) and *The Goslings* (1924), and the oil industry in *Oil* (1927).

In 1937, Sinclair attacked Henry Ford and his corporation at a time when a new labor organization, the United Automobile Workers, was initiating its organizational campaign against the massive Ford enterprise. The young UAW had just mounted and won a monumental struggle against General Motors in the famous Flint sit-down strikes in the winter of 1936-1937. After this classic labor-management confrontation, the robust and confident UAW decided to undertake a major union drive against the Ford Motor Company. The UAW used *The Flivver King* as part of this campaign. The initially unsuccessful organizational effort received notoriety in the infamous "Battle of the Overpass,'' where Walter Reuther, a young and talented UAW leader, and other organizers were set upon by thugs from the Ford Service Department. This incident helped to tarnish Ford's favorable reputation.

In the first two decades of the twentieth century, Ford's reputation was awe-inspiring. Like Thomas Edison and Andrew Carnegie, he was one of the truly legendary and mythic figures of American popular culture. All were transitional figures whose lives spanned the gulf between the less complex world of preindustrial towns and workshops and the sophisticated modern world of urban industrial capitalism. In the popular mind, Henry Ford was the farm boy who went to the city and made good. His life mirrored the Horatio Alger tale—spunk, discipline, and hard work, with its rewards of upward social mobility and economic gain. When he left the country for the city, he became a skilled machinist and later an engineer for the Detroit Edison electric company. As one of the numerous part-time tinkerer-craftsmen of his day, he invented one of the many early automobiles in the 1890s. Soon afterwards, he demonstrated his entrepreneurial talents by forming the Ford Motor Company. Eventually he acquired full ownership of the firm as his personal family enterprise and he became the world's first billionaire.

But Henry Ford was much more in the American mind. He was the technological revolutionary who gave the world the assembly line and modern mass production. John D. Rockefeller proclaimed the Ford Highland Park factory the "industrial marvel of the age." Ford was also touted as the "social revolutionary" who paid his workers the then-unheard-of sum of five dollars a day. His high-wage policy resulted in condemnation and acclaim from the most unlikely quarters. Industrialists condemned Ford as a "traitor to his class" for undermining the prevailing wage rates. And a number of Socialists (circa 1913-14) hailed Ford as the true friend of the American workman. So enduring was the Ford legend that a 1940 Roper survey of American workers ranked Henry Ford as the American leader who was "most helpful to labor."

Nonetheless, Ford's inauguration of "the machine age" did produce its critics. Notable among these were Charlie Chaplin, whose classic film *Modern Times* successfully assailed the degradation of mechanized work, and Aldous Huxley, whose *Brave New World* dated the modern era from "the year of our Ford," when the Model T and its assembly lines originated. Upton Sinclair's *Flivver King* just as eloquently and much more directly developed a sharp critique of the impact of Fordism.

Structurally, *The Flivver King* examines two social worlds—the Ford family and the Shutt family, the successful world of the rising industrialist and the precarious world of the working class. On the one hand, Sinclair's depiction of Ford's life is quite factual, based on Ford's ghost-written autobiographies, company publications and newspaper accounts. Sinclair the novelist, of course, fleshed out his story of Ford with fictionalized scenes. On the other hand, his description of the Shutt family is purely fictional, but reflects an acute awareness of the character of workingclass life and culture of the period. Throughout the novel, Sinclair paints a picture of Ford's meteoric rise to the social heights of urban industrial life in tandem with three generations of the Shutt family, whose fortunes partially rise with Ford's. However, the Shutts' workingclass fate is also far more unsettled and far more dependent on the booms and busts of the business cycle. In good times, the Shutts gain a modest margin of comfort and respectability, but in hard times their fragile world shatters in fragments of economic insecurity and personal despair.

*The Flivver King* begins with a young boy's first introduction to the "crazy" inventor of the 1890s. Young Abner Shutt starts his and his family's complex relationship with the Ford family. As the boy approaches manhood, Ford personally recommends him for his first real job in the new Ford Motor Company in the early 1900s. From here on, bound to the success of the Ford enterprise, Shutt gratefully harnesses his fortunes to the great Henry Ford, moving from humble "spindle-nut screwer" to "full-fledged sub-foreman of spindle-nut screwing." In the process, he moves up the social ladder to a semblance of workingclass economic security. Through the years, he witnesses the great changes in the Ford empire: the introduction of the Model T, popularly known as the "tin lizzie" or "flivver"; the mechanization of production and assembly in the Highland Park plant; and the formation of Ford's entirely new system of labor relations.

In contrast to many Ford biographers and historians, Sinclair accurately depicts the essential outlines of the Ford experience. Henry Ford's vision of the standardized Model T, his "motor car for the great multitude," revolutionized industrial practice in the nation and in the world. The development of the single and unchanging automobile model meant the possibility for the creation of an industrial system for the production of that novel product in 1908. At the turn of the century, American mechanical engineers had produced a new class of machine tools: single-purpose machines. These new devices, embodying the skills of metal-working craftsmen, rapidly turned out large quantities of nearly identical interchangeable parts. With a single model to produce, Ford managers and engineers could readily invest in such costly machines and achieve enormous savings in their manufacturing operations. Around the same time, Ford managers adopted Frederick W. Taylor's ideas on "scientific management." They effectively "Taylorized" work routines—that is, divided and subdivided work tasks into smaller and smaller fragments throughout the plant.

Additionally, when the inexpensive Model T proved its popularity, Ford realized another opportunity with the construction of a brand new plant in Highland Park in 1910. He could design a whole new factory around the manufacture of the Model T. As they moved machines to the new plant, Ford engineers experimented with their arrangement and layout. They came upon the idea of "progressive production," the sequential placement of machine tools to suit the manufacture of parts for Ford automobiles. Instead of the traditional grouping of machines according to their class (*i.e.*, drill presses, lathes, milling machines, etc.) they arranged them to follow the flow of production. This progressive production contained the seed of the idea of the assembly line. By 1913, Ford engineers began their experimentation with the "progressive assembly" of automobile parts and components. The result was the modern assembly line, first for small components such as the magneto and later for the final assembly of the entire automobile. In the end these innovations resulted in the new conception of the huge Highland Park plant as a gigantic clockwork mechanism for the production of Ford automobiles. Materials, men and machines created a large mechanical organism, thoroughly integrated and fully synchronized. Each separate part moved along its predetermined path in the factory. Tiny trickles of parts flowed into small streams of components which flowed into larger rivers of larger components which in turn flowed into the main estuary of final assembly.

Remarkably efficient for the production of the Ford automobile, this new industrial efficiency was ruthless in its impact on the social world of work. The most significant social consequence of Ford mass production was the restriction of work at machines or assembly lines to repetitive and meaningless motions, a phenomenon accurately portrayed in Chaplin's *Modern Times*. The new industrial system established what modern social critics have labeled "work and its discontents" and "the degradation of work."

Ford mass production also transformed the social structure of modern industry and indeed, of modern society. The specialized machines and the Taylorized work tasks destroyed the forms of skill which had long existed in metal-working shops and plants. Early Ford shops had relied on the complex and varied skills of mechanics, skilled machinists, molders, blacksmiths and other craftsmen. With the establishment of the Highland Park plant, the deskilled machine operator and unskilled assembler became the most common figures in the automobile plant.

Finally, Ford's new industrial system required new forms of control for the workforce. Management assumed a greater role in the supervision and direction of workers in the shops and departments. More important, mass production brought with it additional technical controls which reduced workers' discretionary activities. The machinist was controlled by the monotonous routine of his special-purpose machine, reduced to emptying and filling it as the machine worked automatically. The assembler was limited by the subdivision of his task and by the pace of the conveyor when an increase in the speed of the line increased output.

This social and technical transformation of the workplace changed the character of the workers who filled the deskilled jobs on the production and assembly lines. Formerly, highly skilled German and American craftsmen predominated in the Ford shops. Now, however, since almost anyone could perform the simple new work tasks, large numbers of unskilled workers, many of them immigrants, swarmed into the rapidly expanding Ford factory. These new workers had not been habituated to the industrial discipline required by so integrated a factory system. Moreover, workers generally resisted the new brutal regimen. In 1913, absenteeism averaged 10 percent a day in the new Ford factory. During the same year, labor turnover, or the quit rate, amounted to an astounding 370 percent. Such figures testified to an enormous labor problem in the new Ford plant. To maintain the daily workforce—almost 14,000 at the time—Ford employment officials had to hire an extra 1400 workers to keep the interconnected system in operation. To maintain the work force through the year, they had to hire almost 52,000 new workers. The labor problems of mechanized production formed an extraordinary management problem for Ford officials.

These problems were the social reasons underlying the famous "melon" for Ford workers—the five-dollar day. Sinclair, in *The Flivver King,* was directly on target with his description of the famous Ford wage-reform and its less familiar accompanying feature, the Sociological Department. In his effort to induce workers to remain in the plant and to work under the routinized and monotonous conditions, Ford had to increase the financial return to his workers. Although some workers resisted such routinization, many, like Abner Shutt, fueled by aspirations for a better life, accepted the trade-off of high wages for degraded work. However, the inducement was much more than a simple high-wage policy.

Ford's Sociological Department attempted to remake workers in conformity with the requirements of the new industrial system and to instill them with the Ford vision of the good life. The famous five-dollar day was a sophisticated profit-sharing scheme to adapt workers to the Ford shops. For the unskilled worker, who earned about $2.40 per day in wages, Ford officials added about $2.60 per day in profits. All workers were entitled to their wages, but only "qualified" workers received their profits. The general qualifications included living with and supporting one's family, good home conditions, good habits and thrift. The specific conditions encouraged a ford image of middle-class values and life-style for Ford workers. The emphasis was on hard work, self-discipline, cleanliness, sobriety, thrift and "Americanism" for the thousands of immigrant workers in the Highland Park plant. A staff of sociological investigators went to workers' homes and interrogated family, friends and neighbors for their evaluation of Ford workers. Those who conformed to Ford standards were rewarded with the five-dollar day. Those who did not were advised to mend their ways or face dismissal and replacement by any one of the thousands who waited at the plant gates for one of the lucrative Ford jobs.

In the short run, the Ford profit-sharing plan worked because Ford could pay and could feed workingclass aspirations for social and economic improvement. But in the long run it failed, because the cycle of technical advantage eventually gave way to one of bitter economic competition. As the new industrial methods diffused through Detroit's automobile industry, Ford lost the advantage of his technological innovations.

Additionally, a new social toughness emerged during World War I and the post-war labor upsurge in 1919. The world war generated an hysterical anti-Prussian outburst on the part of American public opinion, and the 1919 strike wave sustained a similar outburst against Bolshevism. In this social climate, industrial espionage supplanted sociological reformism as the keystone in Ford labor policy. The outlines of the "American Plan," a hardline anti-labor policy, emerged in the post-war period as the notorious Harry Bennett's star rose in the Ford constellation. In the 1920s, the Ford Service Department replaced the reform-oriented Sociological Department. Instead of sociological investigators and advisors, Bennett's thugs harassed, intimidated and brutalized independent-minded Ford workers through labor's "lean years." Although Ford workers prospered in the 1900s and 1910s, during a phase of technical innovation, they fell back into social and economic insecurity in the 1920s and

'30s, during a phase of economic competition and decline. The speed-up, the stretchout, demotions, low wages, short workweeks with pay reductions, and intermittent periods of underemployment and unemployment became more frequent for Ford workers all through the 1920s. Then, following the long shutdown in 1927 to retool for the Model A, came the social catastrophe of 1929, the onslaught of the Great Depression, shattering the hopes and dreams of thousands of Ford workers. It was in these changed conditions that the usually cautious Abner Shutt began to think critically of his generous master, especially after the murder of four Ford workers who took part in the Ford Hunger March in 1932.

The most remarkable feature of *The Flivver King* is Sinclair's sensitivity to the condition of the American worker—his compassion for the harsh realities of workingclass existence. This is well revealed in his fascination with the social basis of workingclass conservatism. Perhaps, as a beleaguered American socialist in a society generally unsympathetic to the plight of the less fortunate, Sinclair pondered the classic question of the failure of socialism to gain a solid and enduring foothold among American workers. He seems to have recognized that dreams of social and economic stability, if not prosperity, were strong drives among American workers. The possibilities of a better life for themselves or for their children meant an escape from the cruel economic realities of the workingclass world.

Thus Abner Shutt expresses grateful appreciation for Ford's recommendation for work in the new automobile company. This appreciation, in addition to his personal success within the plant hierarchy, cements his fortunes to Henry Ford and his company. Through thick and thin, through good times and bad, Shutt remembers only the positive dimension of his relationship to Ford. Shutt's children strive to achieve economic security and to escape the world of their father. The oldest, John, chooses the familiar workingclass path of technical education and becomes a salaried manager in the Ford factory. Hank, named after the great benefactor, is the problem child. Enticed by the easy money of organized crime in the freewheeling era of Prohibition, he eventually ends up as a factory spy in the Ford Service Department. Daisy, the only daughter, selects another common avenue of escape, the lower-middle-class route of a clerical occupation and marriage to a bookkeeper. Tom, the bright high-school athlete, goes to the state university with the offer of an athletic scholarship. For a while, all achieve a modicum of economic security during the boom years, but their fortunes decline during the Great Depression. Only Hank's skills are required to forestall the organizational efforts of discontented Ford workers. Tom, who is radicalized in college and becomes a UAW organizer, alone retains his social identity and his sense of worth.

In retrospect, the ambiguity of *The Flivver King*'s pessimistic conclusion is rather disconcerting. Of course, Sinclair could not predict the outcome of the UAW's Ford unionization campaign. Perhaps the formidable Ford empire and its brutal opposition to labor were sufficient reasons for the novel's uncertain end. Or perhaps in the course of his embattled years, Sinclair's vision of the future of industrial America had become embittered. In any case, sometimes even the real world has its happy endings. Four years after the novel appeared, the UAW proved victorious against the Ford empire.

Stephen Meyer

*Department of Humanities*
*Illinois Institute of Technology*

# *SELECTED BIBLIOGRAPHY*

Sidney Fine, *Sit-Down: The General Motors Strike of 1936-1937.* Ann Arbor, 1969.

Henry Ford, *My Life and Work.* Garden City, New York, 1922.

Stephen Meyer, *The Five Dollar Day: Labor Management and Social Control in the Ford Motor Company, 1908-1921.* Albany, New York, 1981.

Allan Nevins, et. al, *Ford: The Man, The Times, The Company.* New York, 1954.

————, *Ford: Expansion and Challenge.* New York, 1957.

Joyce Shaw Peterson, "Autoworkers and their Work, 1900-1933," *Labor History,* V. 22 (Spring, 1981), pp. 213-36.

————, "Autoworkers Confront the Great Depression, 1929-1933," *Detroit in Perspective,* V. 6 (Fall, 1982), pp. 47-71.

Keith Sward, *The Legend of Henry Ford.* New York, 1972.

# THE
# FLIVVER KING

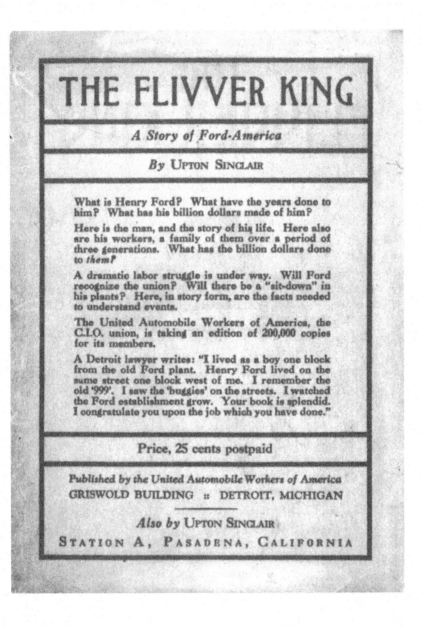

# THE FLIVVER KING

*A Story of Ford-America*

*By* Upton Sinclair

What is Henry Ford? What have the years done to him? What has his billion dollars made of him?

Here is the man, and the story of his life. Here also are his workers, a family of them over a period of three generations. What has the billion dollars done to *them?*

A dramatic labor struggle is under way. Will Ford recognize the union? Will there be a "sit-down" in his plants? Here, in story form, are the facts needed to understand events.

The United Automobile Workers of America, the C.I.O. union, is taking an edition of 200,000 copies for its members.

A Detroit lawyer writes: "I lived as a boy one block from the old Ford plant. Henry Ford lived on the same street one block west of me. I remember the old '999'. I saw the 'buggies' on the streets. I watched the Ford establishment grow. Your book is splendid. I congratulate you upon the job which you have done."

Price, 25 cents postpaid

Published by the United Automobile Workers of America
GRISWOLD BUILDING :: DETROIT, MICHIGAN

*Also by* Upton Sinclair
STATION A, PASADENA, CALIFORNIA

Cover of the first edition (1937)

# I

"Mom," said little Abner, "there's a feller down the street says he's goin' to make a wagon that'll run without a hoss."

"He's crazy," said Mom.

"He don't look like he's crazy," argued the boy. "He looks like a nice feller."

"Well, you keep away from him. You don't want to go foolin' round no cranks."

It wasn't the first time that mothers had been mistaken as to what their children wanted. All the boys in the neighborhood wanted to see the "horseless carriage," and hear what the feller had to say about it. One of his ways of being "nice" was liking to talk to kids; their minds were less fixed in the notion that because something never had happened, therefore it never could happen. On warm summer evenings, when he worked with the door of his shed open, there would be several boys in the entrance looking on; if they behaved themselves and asked smart questions, he didn't mind if they came inside and watched his work. He would explain the idea of a new kind of engine, in which the fire, instead of being built underneath a boiler, was inside a metal cylinder, the power coming from a series of gas explosions, small but very fast.

Abner said no more to his mother about it, because the word "explosion" would send her into a panic. After supper he ran out to play with the other kids, and if instead of chasing cats and pulling girls' pigtails they listened to explanations about internal combustion engines, what harm was there? It was something you didn't have in every residence neighborhood, and some of the kids would brag about it, and there were fist-fights over the question whether or not a wagon could be made to run of itself.

It was a thing that looked very much like a baby-carriage; that double kind they build when a family is blessed with twins. This one was just big enough for a pair of grown-up twins to sit in side by side, squeezed tight. It ran on four bicycle wheels with solid rubber tires, and in front was a handle, like the tiller of a boat, which you pushed, as in a boat, opposite to the way you wanted to go.

Below and behind the seat was this new and queer kind of engine. For many months the inventor had it up on his work-bench, where he could tinker at it and add new parts. It had two cylinders, made out of gas pipe, two and a half inches in diameter. Each cylinder had a piston, closely fitted, and a device by which a drop of gasoline was let inside and exploded by an electric spark. When the engine

3

was started, it made a racket like what was known as a gatling-gun; it gave out a grey smoke of disagreeable odor, which caused the inventor to open the door of the barn in a hurry. The neighbors would hear it for a block in every direction, and would say: "There goes that crazy loon again. Some day he's going to blow himself up." If they were extra nervous they would say, "He's going to blow us all up," and wonder why the police allowed such a thing in a respectable neighborhood.

But the kids found it as good as the Fourth of July. They would come running, and stand in the doorway, gaping. The engine shot out a series of quick bright sparks, delightful to watch. It was generally at night, because this Mr. Ford worked for the electric company in the day-time. Every night he worked until late, apparently having no other interest in the world. On Saturday nights he worked until ungodly hours—a literal statement, since never before had this neighborhood known of a man's working at machinery on Sunday.

The engine caused a shaft to spin round and round, so fast that you could hardly see it moving. Mr. Ford had it figured out that if he hitched that up to the axles of the baby-carriage, it would push the thing; every now and then he would proceed to hitch it up and try. But there would be something wrong, and he would have to take it off and tinker some more. He was always ready to explain about it, being a talkative young fellow, and not seeming to have any secrets. Yes, sir, he was going to make a baby-carriage that would run of itself, and better than any other man's baby-carriage.

You would see the roads full of them; in the end there would be no more horses. The kids would go off and argue about it, for or against.

In the end the neighborhood got used to this eccentric inventor, even his failure to remember the Lord's day. But none of them took any stock in his notion that he would ever climb up a hill without any creature to haul him. Men were used to heavy steam-engines moving on rails; but to go running loose on a public highway without something hitched in front was contrary to nature, if not to law. It was almost as silly as the efforts some other men were making to fly in the air.

## II

Abner's father was named Shutt, and worked in a big factory where they made railway freight-cars. His job was bolting timbers of these cars together; it was rated as semi-skilled work and was well-paid, he averaged as high as a dollar-forty a day. But also it was hard work, and even though he was a tough man who had labored all his life, after a ten-hour day he was exhausted, and sometimes fell asleep in the street-car on the way home, and went by his stop. He was too tired to read an evening newspaper, and rarely stayed up more than an hour after supper on week-days.

Tom Shutt and his family lived in one side of a two-family frame house on the street in back of Mr. Ford's shed. The house had been painted white, but so long ago that no one could remember. There was a parlor and kitchen downstairs, and upstairs two bedrooms, in one of which slept Tom and his wife, with their little girl, and in the other Abner and his three older brothers. There was running water in the kitchen, but the toilet was in a little house in the back yard. This was a hardship in winter, but they didn't know it, having never heard of any other arrangement.

In the other half of the house lived the O'Rourke family, with nine children, and they were fighting Irish. Mr. O'Rourke got drunk every Saturday night, and came home and beat his family; you could hear it just as if it were in the same room with you. It was hard for an American and Protestant family to get used to, but Mrs. O'Rourke made it plain that she would rather be beaten than have aliens interfere in her affairs. It was the blessing of the Shutt family that the father belonged to an evangelical sect, the Original Believers, who had two leading principles, one being total abstinence, and the other being total immersion of adults, each wearing a white robe as in the Bible pictures.

They were poor, but far from hopeless; not only had they the certainty of a blessed state in the hereafter, but the children were all going to school, and the family shared the faith of all American families, that the young ones would rise in the world. America was the land of opportunity, and wonderful things were happening every day. The poorest boy had the right to become president; and beside this grand prize were innumerable smaller ones, senators, governors, judges, and all the kings, lords, and lesser nobility of industry. Life in this land was a sort of perpetual lottery; every mother who bore a child, even in a dingy slum, was putting her hand into a grab-bag, and might draw out a dazzling jewel.

Even toil-battered Tom Shutt knew this. He had a newspaper delivered to his home every Sunday morning, and after he came back from church and had his dinner, he read it until he fell asleep. In this paper he saw pictures of fashionable ladies and fabulously rich and successful men. The papers told how these men had risen from a state of poverty like his own, and that they had done it by producing useful things which had raised the standards of life in America until they were the highest in the world. Every sharer in these bounties felt his heart glow with pride; Tom's glowed as warmly as any —only he wished the boys' shoes didn't wear out so fast, and that the missus didn't have to work so hard patching their pants.

One evening in the late fall, Indian summer and warm, Tom was sitting on the two wooden steps which led to his front door. He still had on his sweaty blue cotton shirt and overalls; the only part of him which was clean was his hands which he had washed for supper. He wore a straggly brown mustache, and several days' growth of beard—for as a rule he only shaved on Sunday mornings. His face was leathery and wrinkled, and wore a patient, ox-like expression. He puffed meditatively on his pipe, full of blessed peace honestly earned.

His freckle-faced kid came from in back of the house and sat by him. "Gee, Pop," said Abner, "you ought to come see that horseless wagon Mr. Ford is makin'. He's got it out in front of the shed."

Now Tom had been hearing about that contraption for half a year, and just then was not too sleepy to feel a stirring of curiosity. "All right, let's have a look." He knocked the ashes from his pipe and let the thirteen-year-old·youngster lead him down the alley to the little red brick barn, or stable, in which the inventor was at work.

Mr. Ford was a lean, thin-faced man of twenty-eight, with wavy brown hair and an alert expression. His workshop was just big enough for one buggy and one horse, with a wide door for the buggy and a narrow one for the horse, and a little square hole for a window. He had cleaned it out and put in a work-bench and an array of tools, and this baby-carriage for grown-up twins. At present the contraption was out in the open, and a couple of boys were having fun pushing it this way and that while Mr. Ford worked the steering-tiller. He seemed to be satisfied with the way this part of it was behaving; there seemed no doubt that if he could make the thing go at all, he could make it go where he wanted it.

When the tests were over, Abner said, "This is my Pop." Mr. Ford nodded politely, and Tom ventured, "That'll be quite an invention if you get it to workin', Mr. Ford."

"Oh, I'm going to get it to working," said the other. "I figured it all out before I started."

"You'd ought to be able to sell it," mused Tom. As a good American, he thought of the business side. "There's a lot of rich folks would amuse theirselves runnin' round in a buggy like that."

"It's not only rich folks, Mr. Shutt," replied the inventor, always ready for conversation. "I'm not making this for a toy, but for real use. I mean to make them wholesale, so that a man like you will have one to drive to his work in."

"Where would a man like me get the money to pay for such a thing, Mr. Ford?"

"Did you ever stop to think how much it costs to get to your work? Suppose it's ten cents a day, that's thirty dollars a year—and for one person. There's no reason a wagon like this shouldn't be built to carry four people at once."

"Well, I dunno, Mr. Ford," murmured Tom. He was a polite and humble man, and he didn't say, "I'll believe it when I see it." He just said: "I wish you luck, sir."

Mr. Ford, who wasn't humble, but argumentative, and full of his ideas, replied: "Not luck, Mr. Shutt; science and calculation. I've reasoned this thing out, and I know what I can do. You wait and see!"

### III

This was on Bagley Street in the city of Detroit; quite a large city, and an old one, as age goes in America. It stood on the river which joins Lake Erie with Lake St. Clair, and steamers came from long distances. Across the river was Canada, and several railroads came through, and there was a lot of manufacturing, and shipping of products in and out. This young fellow, Henry Ford, was doing his own manufacturing, in back of the cottage in which he lived with his wife.

It was 1892, and all that year he had spent his spare time and money on his invention. He had started work as a machinist with the electric company at forty-five dollars a month, but he wasn't quite as poor as that, for his father was a farmer, and had given him forty acres of land on which he had built a sawmill. He had worked hard all his life, and learned all he could find out about machinery. He carried in his pocket a watch which he had made with two dials, one to show the sun-time which the farmers were used to, and the other the new time brought in by the railroads. Back on the farm was a steam-engine, intended to haul a plow; the ingenious young man had built it of old rusty parts of various broken-down agricultural implements.

The year passed, as years have a way of doing, without horses to pull them or engines to drive them. There came a cold winter, and still Mr. Ford tinkered in his shed, with a little wood stove to warm him. Now and then he would try the contraption, but there was always something wrong. It had a wooden fly-wheel, and its transmission was a leather belt, and neither was proof against accidents. Its ignition depended upon a series of electric sparks, and to get those correctly timed was not so easy. As fast as one problem was solved, others developed.

But in the month of April there came a burst of strenuous effort; the inventor worked two days and nights without rest or sleep, and at two o'clock in the morning came in to tell his wife that the machine was ready, and he was about to make a test. It was raining, and she came out under an umbrella to see what happened.

There was a crank in front, and you had to turn it over to start the engine. It made a mighty sputtering, then a roaring, and shook the vehicle most alarmingly; but it held together, and Mr. Ford got in and started. He had a kerosene lamp in front, and by this dim light went down the street paved with cobble-stones. Mrs. Ford stood in the rain for a long time, wondering if she would ever see her husband again. There was no way to reverse the engine, and if he was in a narrow street he had to get out and lift the rear end around.

The young inventor was gone a long time, and came back pushing the contraption. A nut had come loose, with all the shaking. But he was exultant; in spite of bumpy cobble-stones and muddy ruts, he had gone where he wished to go. "You're wet through," said his wife, and he let her lead him into the kitchen, and take off his wet things and hang them up, and give him hot coffee. He was talking excitedly all the time. "I've got a horseless carriage that runs!" said Henry Ford.

## IV

The young inventor continued to tinker, and to make improvements in his invention, until finally he gained confidence enough to take it out in daylight. Then began a series of excitements; for the streets of Detroit were full of horses, which saw in this carriage their ultimate exterminator, and their one idea was to get as far from it as possible. They would turn, regardless of shafts or wagon-tongues, and bolt for the open spaces. The drivers denounced the contraption as a "devil wagon", and became so threatening that Mr. Ford went to the mayor of the city and got a permit to drive a horseless carriage; for a time he could boast of being the only licensed chauffeur in the United States.

It was summer-time, and school was over, and here was a show for the boys of the neighborhood. The moment

Abner Shutt heard the gatling-gun start shooting, he would dart from his home; a troop of others would join him, and follow the smoky trail of the fire-wagon. It went about as fast as the boys could trot comfortably; but they had an advantage, in that they could leap over the holes in the paving. When the machine stopped, there were plenty of assistants to turn it around. If it quit entirely, they would help to push it home—Abner did this once, and it was something he would talk about all the rest of his life.

Having to be pushed home was a common experience to Mr. Ford. It developed that a gas engine had a tendency to melt itself after it had been driven a mile or two; so it was necessary to devise a water-jacket. Then there had to be a pump to circulate the water and a fan to cool it. There seemed no limit to the complications involved in replacing those natural machines known as horses and bicyclists!

The bicyclists took to following the contraption in droves; they would ride alongside and express their opinions of the inventor. If he stopped without wishing to, they would yell: "Get a horse!" If he stopped intentionally, they would surround him and stare. If he went away and left the carriage, somebody would get in and try to start it; finally he had to get a chain and lock, and fasten one wheel to a lamp-post.

The newspapers of course took up the contraption, and had a hard time deciding how to treat it. Was a horseless carriage a joke, or was it a step in civilization? Mr. Henry Ford presented a serious and respectable figure; he never went without his derby hat, a little round black dome on top of his head; often his pretty young wife rode by his side, to show how safe and pleasant it was. So the newspapers for the most part treated him politely, and when a bicyclist tried to get under his machine, they did not say much about it. But none of the business men took seriously the idea that this new vehicle might have commercial possibilities; not even when the inventor sold his first one for two hundred dollars, and built another, lighter, and able to run faster with less noise.

Mr. Ford made good in the electric company; they offered to make him general superintendent—but upon condition that he would give up these foolish efforts to introduce "gasoline buggies". The electric company was committed to the idea that electricity was the power of the future; the gas-engine was regarded as incompatible with sound morality. Mr. Ford's answer was to resign his position and give all his time to his crazy idea. He felt that he had to hurry, because several men in different parts of the country were working at the same invention. They did not know one another, but every now and then they would read in the papers how some driver of a horseless carriage had blown himself up, or had tumbled into a ditch, or had succeeded in driving a mile and getting back home.

## V

Painful events took Abner Shutt out of the neighborhood of Mr. Ford's invention. In the summer of 1893 there was a panic in Wall Street, about which Abner knew nothing. But in the course of the winter he began to hear about people losing their jobs, and not being able to find others; it was something known as "hard times"; a natural phenomenon like winter itself, mysterious, universal, cruel. The railroads of the country stopped buying freight-cars; so one day Tom came home in the morning, with the news that the plant had shut down, and his dollar-forty a day was at an end. Very soon two of the older boys had the same experience, and there was the family, completely stranded; in a few weeks their meager savings were used up, and they fell behind with their rent, and had to sell the greater part of their belongings, move the rest into one tenement room, and subsist on the bitter bread of charity.

From the huge lottery-wheel of life, some boys draw lucky years, and grow up in times of peace, and have a chance for happy lives. Others grow up to find it is war-time; they are dragged from their homes, marched into battle, and shot to pieces. It was the fate of little Abner Shutt to be fourteen years old in a time of "trade depression", so he did not get quite enough to eat, and his growth was stunted, and he had to leave school and go out on the streets to earn a few pennies selling newspapers. Every corner was occupied by boys who considered they had a right to it, so Abner was chased from place to place and beaten, and had his papers torn up. The merciless winds of winter lashed his frail ill-clad figure, and his fingers were so stiff with cold that he could hardly make change when he was able to find a customer. Once his fingers froze, and one of them began to turn dark, and the boy, screaming with pain, had to be taken to a hospital, where a doctor cut it off. So Abner

had a souvenir of "hard times" to carry through life.

There was one lad less to run after Mr. Ford's horseless carriage. Abner had to beg for pennies when he could not earn them; his father had to stand in a breadline with hundreds of starving men, and his toil-worn mother had to wrap a shawl about her shoulders and walk to a distant place to have a tin pail filled with soup. Their church helped them a little, but most of its members were working people who had their own troubles. The resources of the charity societies were stretched beyond endurance; all over America were hunger, cold, and misery.

Such was the boy's life for the next two or three years. He never went back to school, but ran errands and did odd jobs whenever he could find them. When at last business picked up, the older boys got work in the car-factory; the father, whose hair was turning grey, was glad to get a berth as a night-watchman. Abner drove a delivery wagon for a while, then he got work in a factory shed, putting crates together. He managed to keep alive, and to grow up, though he was never as strong as his father. He was rather thin, his shoulders somewhat bowed, and his mouth was a little crooked and had two large teeth in front, like a squirrel's. But he grew a fair mustache like his father, and he had honest grey eyes and a kind disposition. He was, and remained, what the church people called a "good moral boy," and at the proper age he was dressed in a white robe and baptized according to the proper formula.

He was taught his father's faith in his country and its institutions, and in spite of all poverty and tribulations, he kept that faith all his life. All the nations had hard times, the newspapers assured him; it was a law of nature and there was no way to escape it. But now prosperity was coming back, and America remained the greatest country in the world, and the richest; if you worked hard, and lived a sober and God-fearing life, success was bound to come to you. There were grumblers and agitators in the land, who blamed conditions on the politicians, or the rich, or anyone except themselves; Abner met one now and then, but in spite of all they could say he continued to look upon the government of his country as he did upon his God, as something remote and sublime, to be adored, even though it might slay him. He became a good Republican, and voted for "protection and prosperity" to the last of his voting days.

## VI

For eleven years from the time he left the farm and came to Detroit to live, Henry Ford was never without some sort of horseless carriage in his workshop. All his spare money went to buying parts, and his spare time to solving problems. He built cars with two cylinders, then with four; he sold them, and they ran, and he saw to it that they continued to run.

Also he tried experiments with the business world and with business men; but he never had much success in finding men to share his ideas. The business people wanted to make money out of selling horseless carriages, and as they saw the problem, it was to find some well-to-do person who could afford an expensive toy; they had to find out exactly what kind of toy he wanted,

and build it for him and get his money. That was supposed to end it, and there was a tendency to consider him a nuisance if he came around complaining that his expensive toy was out of order.

But Henry Ford insisted upon looking at the matter from an entirely different angle. The horseless carriage was not a toy for the rich, but a useful article for everybody. It was foolish asking anybody what he wanted, because he had no way to know what he wanted until he saw it. Go ahead and produce a lot of carriages that could be sold at a low price, and that would run and keep on running. This product would advertise itself on the road, and very soon you would be producing them wholesale, and make a fortune without trying. "Who will make a fortune with me?" asked Mr. Ford, and could find no volunteers.

He went in with a group of men who called themselves the Detroit Motor Company. He was chief engineer, but he could not control the selling, or the kind of cars produced; so quickly he became dissatisfied, and went back to his own little shop, the one place where he could have his own way.

These were the days of the bicycle craze, when everybody was riding the streets of Detroit on what were known as "safeties". Everybody talked bicycles, arguing the merits of Columbias and Monarchs and the English Humbers, as against local makes. There were estimated to be ten million bicycles in use in the United States— there was your mass production, argued Mr. Ford, and some day you would see the same thing in horseless carriages, or motor-cars as they were coming to be known.

The various makes of bicycles were

advertised by means of races. The manufacturers would employ professional riders, and pay them big bonuses if they could beat the riders of the other makes. Mr. Ford had no money to pay anybody, but he could drive his car, and so he issued a challenge to a certain Mr. Winton, who was making a car in Cleveland and advertising it widely.

Here was a great event, the first motor-car race. It was held at the Grosse Pointe racetrack, not far from Detroit, and the newspapers played it up. A crowd came, mostly on bicycles; among them a young workingman by the name of Abner Shutt, riding a model known as "Stearn's Yellow Wheel", which after much scrimping and saving he had purchased at second or third hand. He wore a bicycle-cap, but no proper suit; his best Sunday trousers were bound at the ankles by a pair of "bicycle-clips."

Nine years had passed since Abner had watched Mr. Ford tinkering at his first baby-buggy. Abner had never forgotten it, and whenever he saw the inventor riding about the city he would wave to him; when he read in the paper about Mr. Ford's achievements, the young workingman would be proud, because he had been in at the beginning of that affair. Now he leaned over the railing of the race-track, his face red and his mouth wide open, shouting encouragement to his hero. Many people were shouting, and the hero paid no attention, his mind being on a job which might mean fame and fortune, or again might mean accident, even death.

Mr. Winton's car was known as the "Bullet," while Mr. Ford's was just a "Ford." The pistol sounded, and the

motors roared, and away they went; almost at once Mr. Ford was ahead, and he stayed ahead, while the crowd shouted, and Abner Shutt danced with excitement and delight. When the triumph was complete he was one of a hundred who crowded round the inventor, cheering. Mr. Ford didn't recognize him, or even see him, but Abner got a satisfaction out of announcing to those who stood near: "I uster know that feller when he was makin' his first machine. Sure I did. On Bagley Street, in a little shed." He would have the pleasure of saying that all the rest of his days.

### VII

All Detroit was now convinced that a motor-car could race; but it was still unconvinced that a motor-car was of any real use. Henry Ford went out on the ice in winter, and drove his car a measured mile at a speed of more than thirty miles per hour; he broke the Vanderbilt record, and celebrated it by a muskrat dinner on the ice. But even that didn't cause people to take him seriously. Who but a madman wanted to drive thirty miles per hour?

But they wanted to see races, and Mr. Ford decided to show them a real one. He and a friend built a car just for speed, with four cylinders and eighty horsepower. They tried it out, and it was like "going over Niagara Falls." Mr. Ford himself didn't care for the experience, so they sent for a bicycle-racer by the name of Barney Oldfield, a mad devil who lived on speed. The race-track was not banked at the ends, and getting around the turns was a life and death matter—especially since you had to steer the car with a heavy tiller, that took your two hands to push.

This real "devil wagon" was called "999", and they entered it in the Grosse Pointe races in 1903. Abner Shutt was on hand again, with two fellows who worked with him in the shipping department of a tool factory. It was a three-mile race, and the madcap Barney came in half a mile ahead; Abner danced and shouted, and again told everybody who would listen: "I uster know that Mr. Ford. Sure I did."

When the thrills were over Abner rode his "Stearns Yellow Wheel" back to Detroit, and as they pedalled, he and his friends discussed what had happened, and what they had read in the papers about the different makes of cars. They had been born into an age of speed, and were proud of it. As bicyclists, each swore by his own make, as possessively as if he owned the factory; each was a "scorcher", and made it a point of honor not to let any other rider pass him on the road. And now these motor-driven vehicles were coming upon the scene, so much faster, so much more dangerous and exciting. Young workingmen who had to do with machinery were learning to talk about ignitions and transmissions and cooling systems.

They all agreed that this new business would grow; and in the course of the ride an idea came into Abner's mind: "I wonder if Mr. Ford wouldn't give me a job!"

Abner Shutt had come to a sort of crisis in his life just then. He was twenty-four years of age, and not too sturdy; he had been working at his hard job with the tool company for three years, and had made up his mind that he had no future there. His fore-

man was the sort of fellow who promoted his own friends and those who flattered him and gave him presents. Abner didn't understand the arts of advancing himself—having been taught in Sunday school and in the newspapers that the way to get on was to work hard and faithfully.

Five years ago romance had entered the rather drab and laborious life of Abner Shutt. Her name was Milly Crock, and her parents were working people, members of the Original Believers' Church. Milly was fair-haired with lovely bright blue eyes; she was somewhat frail, but Abner didn't know it; to him she seemed the most wonderful of created things, and very much too good for an ugly graceless fellow like himself. He could hardly believe it, but little by little it became apparent that she favored him; they began meeting at all the social affairs of the church, and then Abner found the courage to call upon her at her home. They were both of them guileless and very shy, and it took a long time for Abner to find out how to ask for her hand. When it was all settled, he had the happiest moments he had ever known.

But they had no money, and they could not marry. They must work and save; and now, at the end of five years, they were still doing it. They were getting tired of hopes deferred; without understanding it exactly, they were possessed by an urge to contribute their share of increase to the fast-growing population of Detroit. It was the time of Teddy Roosevelt, idol of the common man and fiery combater of "race suicide." Business was booming—everybody was getting rich, it seemed to Abner Shutt, except Abner himself.

Such were the impulses driving in the young workingman, as he rode his bicycle home from the races. "I've got to better myself!" he was saying over and over; and he added: "I'll go and see Mr. Ford." He thought it wiser not to mention this bright idea to his two companions.

## VIII

Mr. Ford, as it happened, was also at a crisis of his life just then. He was forty, and had as yet had no business success. He was still making cars almost with his own hands, and seeing other people forge ahead of him. Interest in the idea was spreading, factories were being set up—but he was left out of it.

It happened that among his friends was a coal-dealer named Malcolmson, who had sold coal to the electric company when Henry Ford had charge of its purchases. The coal-dealer had ridden in the Ford car, and been exposed to the Ford enthusiasm; after the stunning triumph of Barney Oldfield, he announced himself a convert, and proposed that he and his friend should organize the Ford Motor Company, and divide between them fifty-one percent of its shares, which would give them control. Malcolmson put up seven thousand dollars to cover the organizing costs. Others were persuaded to invest; the coal-dealer's clerk, whose name was James Couzens, scraped together a thousand dollars, and the bookkeeper did the same. A carpenter whose shop was to be rented came in, and two men, the Dodge brothers, who owned a machine-shop,

agreed to furnish motors for the new cars, and take their payment in stock. Two young lawyers were called in to draw the contract, and they also took a chance.

Altogether the new company started business with $28,000 in cash. None of the great captains of American industry was represented, nor the master minds of finance; the chance of furnishing the American people with a cheap horseless carriage was taken in great part by men who borrowed the money on their wages, and did it because they knew Henry Ford, or had friends who knew him.

It wouldn't have done Abner Shutt any good to know about it, because he had less than a hundred dollars to his name, and didn't know what a stock company was. He didn't even know where Mr. Ford had moved to, or how to get that information. It was just by good luck that he was riding his bicycle on Mack Avenue, and saw a two-story frame building with a new sign: Ford Motor Company.

It was the shop which Mr. Ford was renting from the carpenter, one of his investors, for seventy-five dollars a month. The building had an elaborate "false front," that is a front wall going up higher than the roof, to make you think the place was taller than it was. But it didn't fool you, because as you approached along the street, you saw that the front did not continue at the sides. There were many false fronts like that, in buildings and elsewhere in America.

## IX

Abner alighted and parked his bicycle against the curb. Mr. Ford was there; he was there at practically all hours—and not warming the seat of a swivel-chair, but out in the shop, seeing that production was going along. Abner waited respectfully, cap in hand, until there seemed to be an opening. Then he stepped forward.

"Mr. Ford, my name is Abner Shutt. You don't remember me, but I was one of the kids that uster come and watch you in the shop on Bagley Street. Onst I helped to push your car home when she quit."

"Indeed, Abner," said the other. "I think I remember you. How are you getting along?"

"Not so very good, Mr. Ford. I got a job with Perfection Tool, and I work as hard as a feller can, but I don't get promoted, and I ain't got no future there. I know this business o' yourn is goin' to grow, Mr. Ford, and I'd like a whole lot to work for you."

"Know much about machinery, Abner?"

"A good bit, Mr. Ford, I picked it up here and there. I ride a bike, and hafter tinker with it. I been readin' about your car, and what's in it. I been to the races—I seen you beat Mr. Winton, and the Barney Oldfield race. I sure was proud of you." Then, seeing the other smile, Abner added, hastily: "I'm a good worker, Mr. Ford. I don't never drink, and I come to work regular. If you would give me a chance, I'd do all I know how to satisfy you. I remember how kind you was to all us kids—"

There came a severe look on the inventor's face. He was now vice president and general manager of a company, carrying a heavy responsibility. "We're not starting a charitable enterprise here, Abner. We're going to make cars, and a lot of them. The

men that work for us are going to do real work, and no nonsense about it."

"Oh, Mr. Ford," cried the other, hastily, "I didn't mean nothin' like that! I'm only askin' a chance to work. You won't find no feller in this town that'll work harder, or be more grateful for the chance."

The general manager was appraising him while he talked. He was young, and his eyes were clear, bearing out his statement that he did not drink. Likewise his hands, and the clothing he wore, supported his claim to having worked hard. There was something honest and simple about his face. Skill didn't matter so much to Mr. Ford as willingness to be taught; for the cars he was planning to make were going to be as much alike as possible, and the work was going to be divided so that each man would have only a few tasks.

"All right, Abner," said he, "I'll give you a chance, and if you do as you've promised, you'll be able to better yourself."

"Oh, thank you, thank you, Mr. Ford!" It was the happiest moment of Abner's life. He had decided some time ago that Henry Ford was a great man, and now he was sure of it, and sure that the fortunes of both of them were made.

The employer led him across the crowded shop to a foreman who was just putting on his coat to leave. "Foster, this is Abner Shutt, who I used to know when he was a boy. I want you to take him on and give him a chance to show what he can do. When do you think you can use him?"

"Right away, Mr. Ford, if he wants to come."

"How about it, Abner?"

"I'll come tomorrow, sir. I suppose

I ought to go to my old job and get my time. Will it be OK if I'm here by half past eight?"

"Half past eight it'll be," said the foreman; and Abner thanked them with a fervor which might have touched their hearts, had not their energies been so absorbed with the problems of production.

## X

So Abner Shutt became a cog in a machine which had been conceived in the brain of Henry Ford, and was now in process of incubation. Alone in his shop, Mr. Ford had been free to do what he pleased; but whenever he had gone out among other men and become a part of their organizations, he had been obliged to do what they told him. Now, for the first time in his life, he was going to have an organization of his own; other men were going to obey him, and be shaped according to his ideas.

He was going to do the thinking, not merely for himself, but for Abner —and this was something which suited Abner perfectly. His powers of thinking were limited, and those he possessed had never been trained. If he had had to look around this crowded busy shop and find something to do, he would have been extremely unhappy. But the foreman took him and showed him exactly what to do, and Abner was grateful; all he asked was time to get the hang of it, and after that he would go on doing it, and the less he had to change, the better it would suit him. The new general manager had made a good guess when he acquired this twenty-four-year-old member of the Original Believers' Church.

The place in which Abner went to work was really not a motor-car factory. It had no machines for making parts; practically everything was made outside, on Mr. Ford's specifications, and the former carpenter-shop was merely an assembly plant. It was going to put together a total of 1708 cars in the first year of its existence, which meant about six cars each working day, something hitherto unknown in the new industry. The problem of the general manager was to divide that task into a number of parts, each sufficient to occupy ten hours of a workingman's time, moving as fast as he could be pushed.

In trucks—drawn by horses—came shipments of wire wheels with tires on them. The task which fell to Abner was to go to a shed and get two wheels at a time, and roll them to the car which was nearly finished, and push each wheel onto the axle, and screw on the "spindle-nut" with a wrench. He had to start the threads carefully, and see that he did not deface the nut, and screw it tight enough so that the driver would not some day be tumbled into a ditch and blame the Ford Motor Company. Since Abner had many times taken off and put on the wheels of his bike, he learned this job quickly, and when in his enthusiasm he had shown how fast he could do it, that became the norm, and if ever he fell behind, there would be dark looks and stern questions.

When he knew his job thoroughly, he was shown how to put on the alarm-bell which was placed on the front of each car; also the lantern, bigger than a bicycle-lantern, which was screwed onto the dashboard. These also were bike jobs, and gave Abner no trouble.

Finally he was set to carrying the cushion seats of the car and putting them into place, and wiping the dust from them, and reporting any scratches or imperfections. Such were the tasks which kept him on the move the whole day; but he didn't mind—he was getting seventeen and a half cents per hour, the best he had ever done, and Mr. Ford had promised that if he worked hard, he would be promoted. What more could a workingman ask?

## XI

With this new security in his life, Abner and the blue-eyed Milly Crock summoned their courage, and had a pretty wedding in their white-painted church, and afterwards took a steamer trip, the first and last holiday of their lives. They saw Niagara Falls, and had their photographs taken with the grand spectacle as a background. The portrait took its place in the family album, where their grandchildren would be able to look at it: each of the pair solemn and unsmiling, Milly with puffed sleeves, and Abner with a tight collar, a large made-up cravat, and the ends of his brown mustache twisted to a point and dashingly waxed.

Less than a year later the trusting young couple made their first contribution to the population of their fast-growing city. It was a boy, and they called his name John Crock, after Milly's father. Altogether they had six children, of whom four survived, three boys and a girl; the youngest was named Tom, after Abner's father, and they called him Tommy as long as the old night-watchman lived.

And while Abner and Milly were thus fulfilling their dream, Mr. Ford was occupied with his; to bring it about that when the little Shutts grew up—and likewise the little Smiths and Schultzes and Slupskys and Steins—they should find millions of little horseless carriages available at second-hand prices, to convey them to any place on the land-surface of the globe except a few mountain-tops.

To that end Mr. Ford prowled incessantly about the former carpenter-shop, now crowded with two or three hundred workers. He observed when they bumped into each other, and devised plans to keep them from doing so. He examined materials, read contracts, discussed selling campaigns, and prepared advertisements shrewdly addressed to the mind of the average American, which he knew perfectly because he had had one for forty years. It was his doctrine that no man who wanted to succeed in business should ever let it out of his mind; and he had practiced this half a lifetime before he began to preach it.

In the first year the sales of the Ford Motor Company brought them a million and a half dollars, nearly one-fourth of which was profit. From then on, all his life, Henry Ford had all the money he needed to carry out his ideas. He took care of his money, and used it for that purpose.

The first car, known as Model A, had been sold for $850, and it was Henry's plan to reduce the price, and sell still more cars in 1904. This brought him into conflict with his associates, who clung to the old notion of the motor-car as a plaything of the rich; they wanted to raise the price, and make more fancy models, so that the sales force would have something to talk about. It had come to be with motor-cars as with ladies' hats and dresses; the style had to be changed each year, so that the rich would feel themselves out of fashion, and would hurry to get a new car. The makers were putting onto the back a thing called a "tonneau", a sort of box with two extra seats; one year they put it down low, and the next year they raised it up high; one year you got into it from the back, and the next year from the side. They had picked up in Paris a fancy word, "automobile," and now every winter they had an "automobile show" in New York, where the salesmen flocked to apply pressure to customers.

Henry Ford was willing enough to sell cars at the automobile show, but he wanted to sell them also on Main Street in Oshkosh and Topeka, and was convinced that one thing and one only would do that, a low price. He argued with his associates, but when it came to a showdown, he was outvoted. The Ford Motor Company stopped making Model A at $850, and began making Model C for $900, and Model F for a thousand, and Model B for two thousand. Their sales dropped from 1708 in the first year to 1695 in the second. In the next year they left out the cheapest model, and their sales fell to 1599. They were making progress backwards.

Was it because of the high price, as Henry Ford said, or was it because of the lack of new models, as the salesmen and stockholders insisted? They were sure that his policy meant ruin; but he had no interest in any other policy. He saved his share of the dividends, and took every chance to buy the stock of those who were dissatisfied. First it was the carpenter, Strelow, owner of the shop; he had five thousand dollars in the business, and decided that he would rather put it into a gold-mine. Next it was the turn of the old friend Malcolmson; Henry made up his mind that he couldn't get along with this coal-dealer, and at the end of three years the coal-dealer realized that he couldn't get along with Henry. He sold, and so at last Henry had outright control, and those who didn't agree with his policy got out. From that time on it was the rule of the company that anybody who didn't agree with Henry's policy got out immediately.

The Ford factory made no more touring-cars, as the expensive models were called; it made runabouts and roadsters. Its most expensive car now sold for $750, and there was one as low as $600. The results were immediate; in 1906 they sold more than five times as many cars as in the previous year. Henry Ford had begun his march to fortune.

## XII

While these issues were decided, Abner Shutt was laboring faithfully in the plant; rolling in wheels, sometimes wire ones, sometimes wooden, as the fashion changed, and screwing on spindle-nuts with a righthand thread or a lefthand. He screwed on bells, and later a device which had a rubber bulb, and when you squeezed it there came forth something half way between a toot and a squeak. He screwed on lamps, first kerosene, then a stuff called carbide, for which you had to have a metal cylinder fastened on the running-board. All these various operations Abner performed faithfully, hustling out to the shed to get a couple more wheels, bending his back over the screwing operations, and applying his mind to making sure that he did not put a nut with a righthand thread upon an axle with a lefthand thread.

Now came this new revolution. Of course nobody explained to Abner about stock control and such matters; all he knew was that the models were being changed, there were going to be cheaper cars and more of them. Presently the new stuff began coming in, and first Abner had to work faster, and then it was found that he no longer had time for the horns, and he gave up that job to another man. Production increased still more, and it developed that he no longer had time for lamps. Almost before he realized it, he had become the specialist in spindle-nut screwing of the Ford organization.

One never-to-be-forgotten day Abner summoned his resolution, and waited around the plant after quitting time. He was shaking in his shoes, for Henry Ford was now a heavily burdened man, and if you happened to cross him, or to disturb his mind at an unpropitious moment, he might fall into a violent rage. But Abner had thought it over for a month, and made up his mind. Times were good, and if he was not going to get promotion, one job was the same as another.

So there he was, cap in hand, stepping up to his employer as he came out to his car. "Good evening, Mr. Ford, I am Abner Shutt."

"Hello, Abner!" said the boss, who had a good memory. "How you getting along?"

"No complaints, Mr. Ford. But there's something you had ought to know about the job, if you will let a plain workingman tell you."

It was Mr. Ford's dinnertime, but Mrs. Ford had learned that business always came before pleasure. "What is it, Abner?"

"You're growing fast, Mr. Ford, an' you're goin' on growin'. I hear what people say, an' they all like your car, an' wisht they could buy one."

"Is that so, Abner?" It was the way to the busy man's heart.

"So you're goin' to need more men in my department. An' I see a lot of waste there."

"Waste, Abner? What do you mean?"

"Well, the spindle-nuts come all mixed up, the rights and the lefts. I ain't never spoiled one yet, but somebody will. An' I have to go to the shed for the wheels—they had ought to be brought to me, because screwin' 'em on is skilled work, sorter, an' I could do a lot more of it if I could stay at it. I'm doin' all one man can do, an' if you keep on growin', you'll have to have a man fer the rights and one fer the lefts. It'll be a job by itself, Mr. Ford, puttin' on wheels, an' it ought to be run by a feller that knows, and not jest leave it to guess."

"That sounds all right, Abner. I'll look into it in the morning."

"I been workin' for you three years now, Mr. Ford, an' never missed a day exceptin' that time when I got married. I told you you could count on me, an' you said if I was faithful an' worked hard, I'd better myself. That's what I want to ast you, Mr. Ford"—Abner rushed on breathlessly, for this was his real message, the part that filled him with terror—"Some day you're goin' to hafter have a puttin' on wheels department, an' I want you to know that I've learnt the work, an' proved I can do it, an' can show it to anybody, an' see they do it. So I want to ast you not to put no other feller in there on top o' me—I'd oughter be the foreman or whatever you have there, myself."

So there it was. Mr. Ford wasn't mad, on the contrary, he seemed to think it reasonable, and he said he would look into it, and nobody would be put on top of Abner Shutt. Next day he came, and watched the work for a while—poor Abner's heart thumped so that he could hardly breathe, but fortunately he knew his work so well that he could have done it in his sleep. The result was that the spindle-nuts now came already sorted, and there was a man whose duty it was to bring them, and to roll the wheels in from the shed. Before long Abner was confining himself to putting on rights; and there was another man putting on lefts, and it was a proud Abner who showed him the work.

In due time there came still further progress; there were two gangs screwing spindle-nuts, a right and left in each gang, and again it was Abner who taught the work. Finally—the grandest day of all Abner's life—there were five men, one to watch the other four, to see that they moved fast enough from car to car, and that wheels were delivered to them at the proper moment, and that they did not spoil the threads nor bruise the caps. That most responsible of men was Abner Shutt, full-fledged sub-foreman of spindle-nut screwing for the Ford Motor Company, at two dollars and seventy-five cents per day—could you imagine it?

## XIII

While these events were taking place, Abner and his growing family had been living in the upstairs part of a house, rented from another occupant. Having three boys and a girl, they were badly crowded; this new prosperity, and the assurance of Mr. Ford's protection, gave them courage to dream of a home to themselves. Abner rode about town one Sunday, and found a five-room house which could be rented for nine dollars a month; it had running water and a toilet inside, which seemed to this humble family a new stage of civilization. For several years this became their home.

Henry Ford also was becoming a proud father at this time; his progeny being a three-story brick factory-building on the corner of Piquette and Beaubien streets, paid for entirely out of profits. When the time came to move out of the rented frame carpentershop, which had less than three-tenths of an acre of floor space, into this sumptuous new structure with more than two and a half acres, and with a quarter of a million dollars worth of new machinery in it, Henry Ford was exalted, but hardly more so than his faithful servant. The two of them had seen this thing grow from nothing, and each had done his part in bringing it to pass.

Everything in the new place had been planned in advance; the site of every piece of apparatus marked with chalk on the floor. As fast as work was finished on the last car in the old place, the benches and tools were moved to the new; the men transported themselves, and very soon were at work on new cars in the new place. Henry himself was on hand, overseeing every detail; "snooping around", some people called it, but that was the way he got results. "Hustle up there! Get a move on you! Get production!"— such were the slogans of the plant. You could rest when you got home, but during work hours you were drawing the company's money, and you earned it with your sweat.

Henry Ford went to Florida to attend an auto race in which one of his cars was entered; there was an accident, and a French car was shattered, and he picked up a piece of it, and found it lighter and tougher than anything he had ever had in his hands before. He carried it home and had it examined; it was vanadium steel, a new alloy, having more than three times the tensile strength of the steel being used in America. It was the thing for motor-cars, at any rate for Fords; Henry brought on a man from England who understood about it, and after some difficulties succeeded in getting it made.

It was the beginning of an epoch; cars would be lighter, stronger, cheaper. Let anybody make fun of the Ford car, saying it was made of tin; Henry would not worry. The people were finding out that it ran; they were buying it, and paying cash—and Henry was collecting the cash. "Seest thou a man diligent in his business," said Solomon. "He shall stand before kings." Henry did not often quote scripture, but many of his customers knew it by heart.

## XIV

In the new plant Abner Shutt's job remained that of specialist in spindle-nut screwing. He did not work with his hands, except in case of emergency, or to show somebody how it should be done. He went about from car to car, watching others work. This was before anybody had thought of the idea of an assembly-line or "belt"; cars were built as one built a house, on one spot. Relays of workmen came, bringing new parts to be added, and tools to do it with. It meant a great many men hurrying about, bumping into one another, and every bump appeared in the price of the completed car.

Abner Shutt did his job loyally, but in his secret heart he never ceased to be afraid of it. Except for the higher pay, he would have preferred to carry a wrench and screw a spindle-nut, as in the old days. He dreaded responsibility, and having to think fast. He had never had any idea that human nature was such a troublesome thing, until he had to deal with men, instead of with pieces of metal that were all alike—or if they weren't, it wasn't Abner's fault.

But men would go off and get drunk, and come back to work with headaches and sore tempers. They would fail to keep their minds on what they were doing, and when they were rebuked, they would blame their boss instead of themselves. Abner was naturally an easy-going fellow, and hated to make trouble for anybody; but there was no avoiding it now, for the work had to be right. He had to scold and "raise hell", and if that didn't do any good, to report the man to Mr. Foster, who would fire him. Abner never claimed the right to fire anybody; indeed he never claimed anything more—not even higher pay.

There came another panic in the fall

of 1907, which filled the city with idle and starving men, and taught humility to those who kept their jobs. It cut down the Ford sales slightly, but not much, for this new product was more and more wanted, and among the hundred million people of America there are always some who can buy what they want. Henry Ford, planning tirelessly, would find new ways to give it to them more cheaply. In the year after the panic he produced 6181 cars, a little over three per worker; but within three years he was managing to get thirty-five thousand cars out of six thousand workers.

Of course nobody ever showed these figures to Abner Shutt, and they wouldn't have meant much to him anyhow. In that period, while learning to make twice as many cars for his employer, Abner was getting a fifteen percent increase in wages, and was considering himself one of the luckiest workers in America. And maybe he was, at that. There were breadlines in Detroit for two winters, reminding him of those dreadful years of his boyhood which had weakened him in body, mind, and soul.

## XV

Milly Crock had been, when Abner invited her to marry him, a pretty thing to look at, with bright complexion, laughing blue eyes, and fair hair which needed no curling-tongs. But five years of waiting, followed by six of child-bearing and housekeeping, caused these charms to fade. She had many pains, the cause of which was obscure; and having four children in the house all the time was a strain upon her disposition. Her fifth child was puny,

and the doctor told her she had better not have any more; but he did not tell her how to arrange this—in those days it was not supposed to be ethical. Soon after this fifth child died, a sixth was born, of a dark blue color, and the mother never saw it.

After that Milly began to exhibit an aversion to her husband, and concentrated all her attention upon her little ones. That was hard upon Abner, who had been a good man according to his lights; but he made the best of it —after all, nobody gets everything in this world, and it is the part of wisdom to do your duty and make sure of a better chance in the next. Abner was fond of his children, and would have liked to play with them when he came home; but often he had to listen to Milly's complaints about them, and deal with them according to the injunctions of Holy Writ.

Three boys and a girl growing up ate a lot of food, and wore out much shoe-leather and textiles. Milly cooked and patched and scrubbed and scolded, and waited for the day when these impatiently demanding creatures would be old enough to go to school, and be off her hands for a few hours. Six days a week, in summer's heat or winter's blizzards, Abner got up at five-thirty and slipped into his clothes, carried in coal and kindlings and built the kitchen fire, ate his chunk of fat meat and fried potatoes, drank his hot coffee with a little "condensed milk," and then mounted his bike and rode away to the Ford plant. Whatever the weather, whatever the circumstances at home, he punched his ticket in the time-clock several minutes ahead, and saw that every man and every wrench was in position at the moment when the whistle blew.

Then the leap into life of men and machinery, the clatter and banging. To the visitor it seemed paralyzing to the nerves, but to Abner it was the normal state of labor; he knew every sound by heart, and noticed in a moment if there was any strange and possibly dangerous one. All he asked was that the men should be on time, and likewise the wheels and the spindle-nuts; that no wrench should slip, no nut be dropped, no curses uttered, no growling at him, or at Mr. Ford or his company or his cars; nothing but a steady and proper racket—and when the long day was over, the blessed knowledge that he had earned another three dollars, and at the end of the week would take it to Milly, to be hidden in her capacious stocking, and doled out for rent and gas and fuel and food.

Some persons would not have cared for this life, but Abner didn't know any such persons, and had no contact with their ideas. He did not think of the Ford plant as an immense and glorified sweatshop; he thought of it as a place of both duty and opportunity, where he did what he was told and got his living in return. If you had invited him to pass judgment upon it, he would have been puzzled at first; but finally he would have said that it was a wonderful place, in which more than five thousand separate parts, made of many different materials, and of many sizes and shapes, were put together to make a magical whole, in which a man could ride anywhere except up the side of a wall. If you had asked him to tell you his ultimate dream of happiness on this earth, he

would have answered that it was to have money enough to buy one of those cars—a bruised and battered one, any one so long as it would run, so that he could ride to work under shelter when it was raining, and on Sundays could pack Milly and the kids into it, and take them into the country, where his oldest brother worked for a farmer, and they could buy vegetables at half the price charged at the corner grocery.

## XVI

Henry Ford had by now experimented with eight different models. The first one, Model A, had had a two-cylinder engine placed in back, and a chain drive. One by one these features had been given up; a four-cylinder engine, placed under a hood in front, and with a shaft drive, had become the standard Ford car. In the year 1908 Henry got up the courage to carry out his own idea of concentrating upon a single cheap car for the masses. One day, without any previous hint to his sales force, he announced that Models A, B, C, F, N, R, S, and K were out forever; thereafter the only Ford would be Model T. He closed the subject with his famous remark that "Any customer can have a car of any color that he wants, provided it is black."

It was an ugly enough little creation he had decided upon; with its top raised it looked like a little black box on wheels. But it had a seat to sit on, and a cover to shelter you from the rain, and an engine which would run and run, and wheels which would turn and turn. Henry proceeded upon the theory that the mass of the American people were like himself, caring very little about beauty and a great deal about use. They wanted to be able to get into a car and go places. They might not always know where they wanted to go, or what they would do when they got there—but these were problems which Henry did not have to solve.

The sales force was staggered; the rest of the automobile trade predicted Henry Ford would be on the rocks in six months. His answer was to buy sixty acres of land in a town called Highland Park, some ten miles north of Detroit, and begin the erection of the biggest automobile plant the world had ever seen. He charged $950 for the touring-car that year, and sold more than eighteen thousand of them, and had several millions of profit to pay for land and buildings. Next year he reduced the price of the touring car to $780, and sold twice as many, and had still more millions.

Henry was riding high. He had won his fight, and he was master. He could order men, and they would obey. He could make things, and build machines to make more things. A hundred cars a day was only a beginning, he insisted; presently he would be making a thousand a day; before he finished he would make a million Fords.

He surrounded himself with experts; men who knew metals, and how to smelt them and refine them and combine them and press them; men who knew fuels, and how to produce heats of higher degree at lower cost; men who knew the hundreds of materials that went into a car, or that might go into a car for the first time; men who knew building, management, accounting, transportation, advertising—the thousand and one arts that would help

to make cars, and to sell them, and to get the money, so that he might make more cars and sell them and get more money.

You might laugh as you said that, but you wouldn't trouble Henry. He knew what he was going to do: revolutionize transportation in America, remake its highways, and change the habits of the people. He was going to make them over into people like himself. They would become sober and honest and hardworking, like him; mechanics and lovers of machinery like him; rich—well, possibly not quite so rich as he, but as rich as was good for them. They would have high wages, and be taught to save a part each week —until they had enough to make the first down payment on a Ford Model T roadster that would last them ten years, twenty years—you would see them on the road when Henry's grandchildren were grown up.

All this was beginning there at Highland Park. He was building his own power-plant, his own steel plant, his own forges. Presently he would have his own iron-mines, coal-mines, ships and railroads. It would be a gigantic empire, spreading over the whole earth; and Henry would be the founder of it, the master of it; his spirit would rule it, his wisdom and his common sense. The last was the phrase that he preferred. "I am common sense," said the soul of Henry Ford.

## XVII

Abner Shutt couldn't know all the things that went on in the mind of his masterful employer; but he got hints of them. One way in which Abner represented an advance over his old father was that he brought home a paper every evening, and no matter how tired he was, he read some of it. Every now and then he would read accounts of what was being prepared at the new plant. With some of the other fellows he rode out of a Sunday to look at it, and the rest of the week they would talk about what they had seen.

Most of these men were like Abner, proud of their employer and his success; but a few were jealous, they were natural-born kickers, and had the idea that Henry's prosperity had come out of their hides. As if they could have planned all this business! said Abner. As if they would know what kind of a car to build! "Socialists," he called them, a word he had read in the papers. But he didn't have much idea what the word meant. Talk about politics was not encouraged in the plant. Mr. Ford didn't approve of politics.

At the beginning of this year 1912, while the Ford Motor Company was turning out more than two hundred cars a day, Abner had his first serious illness. He went to bed feeling bad, and woke up with a high fever and dizziness. He struggled out of bed on a below-zero morning, and tried to make the fire as usual; Milly had to help him back to bed and pile the covers on to keep him from freezing. She was in a panic, and rushed out for the nearest doctor, who came and said that Abner had the "grippe", of which there was an epidemic. He was ordered to stay in bed, and told that his life might be the penalty of disobedience.

The doctor gave him medicine, which may have helped his body, but surely did not help his mind. It was eight years now that he had never missed a day in his service to Henry Ford, and dread possessed his soul. Half raving with fever, he made Milly go to the nearest store and telephone to the office to report his illness, and beg that he might not lose his job. Even when the company's agent came, and made sure that he was really sick, and promised that his place would be kept for him, he was only half comforted. He knew enough of the routine in that plant to understand the danger of letting it be known that a man could be dispensed with. If the screwing on of eight hundred spindle-nuts per day could go on for several days without the presence of a sub-foreman, then why waste three dollars?

They had a little money in the savings bank; also Abner belonged to an organization called the APSABS; that is to say, the Advanced Philanthropic Society of American Beavers. They had a rented lodge-room, and banners and plumes and a solemn ritual, and once a month they got away from their wives and smoked cigars and discussed whatever affairs in their town interested them especially. They were factory workers like Abner, and a few small tradesmen; the important thing was they were numerous, and out of their funds would pay a small allowance each week, so that those growing kids could be fed while their father was laid up.

There Abner lay, until nature had cured him, with or without the doctor's aid. He sat in a chair, quite weak for a couple of days, and had time to get acquainted with his children. The oldest boy, John, was seven, and was going to school whenever the weather made it possible; he was a serious and good boy. The second was named Henry Ford, and appropriately enough was very active and hard for his mother to manage. Daisy, the little girl, was fair and delicate, and made Abner think in many ways of his mother. Little Tommy was only three, and it was too early to tell much about him, but he knew that he liked to have his dad cut out paper figures from the newspaper, and he would mark them up with colored crayons in a manner which Abner thought showed talent.

At last he was allowed to go back to work; not riding his bike through heavy snow, but standing in a badly crowded street-car. He was haggard, and looked ten years older, and had to sit down now and then through the day, which was bad for discipline. But the fellows were kind to him, and did nothing to worry him, and gradually his strength came back. But the experience made a deep impression on his mind, bringing back the cruel fears of his boyhood.

He was more than ever grateful to the good and powerful Mr. Ford, who provided him with his safe job, and even paid him a profit-sharing bonus of seven and a half percent upon his previous year's earnings. In Abner's case this came to nearly seventy dollars, and it was a godsend, covering the doctor's bills and other losses. Abner had no chance to tell Mr. Ford how he felt; but apparently Mr. Ford guessed it, for some years later he wrote that when he thought about the thousands of families who were dependent upon his enterprise, there seemed to

him something sacred about the Ford Motor Company.

## XVIII

It was the year of a presidential election. There was a college president by the name of Wilson running on the Democratic ticket, and he tried hard to win Abner away from his staunch Republican principles, making eloquent speeches about "the New Freedom." Abner read some of his golden words in the newspapers; but also he read that hard times came when the Democratic party got in, and he was more afraid of hard times than of any tyrant. The college president was elected—and sure enough, business began to slow up, which was enough to convince Abner for the rest of his life. He rarely talked politics, but he went to the polls and voted for Hughes, Harding, Coolidge, Hoover, Landon —not to mention all the governors, senators and congressmen of the Grand Old Party.

Fortunately hard times affected Henry Ford but little. He put down the price of his car to $600, and sold more than five hundred of them every business day. The next year he put it down to $550, and sold nearly a thousand every business day. That process of lowering prices and increasing sales was going right on, Henry insisted; and the people made it plain that they liked the idea.

Millions of them had suddenly discovered that they wanted to move about and see the world. Their grandfathers had crossed the continent in covered wagons, taking a year to do it; now the grandchildren aspired to cross the same continent in a month, and before many years they would be doing it in a week. The little black beetles were out on all the roads, and were beginning to be known by pet names; they were "flivvers," they were "jitneys," they were "tin Lizzies," or sometimes "Henrys". People were making up funny stories about them; everywhere you went you heard "Ford jokes." The general trend of them was that half a dozen tomato-cans and a bedspring were mistaken for a Ford car, and after they had been repaired they ran perfectly. Every such joke was a free advertisement.

Abner Shutt moved his family out to the neighborhood of the new plant; wherever the master went, they would follow. Abner was still in charge of the screwing on of spindle-nuts, and you could believe that a man who had to see four thousand nuts screwed on every day had some job. The plant was so big now that no workingman saw much of what was going on; but he heard about it, in one way or another, and it was like being on hand at the creation of the world. God said, Let there be light, and there was light. Henry said, Let there be flivvers, and one of the "Ford jokes" told about a man who went through the Highland Park plant, and came out scratching his hair, exclaiming: "Seems like I feel those little things crawling all over me!"

## XIX

The manufacturers of automobiles were confronting a problem. The more men they had working, the more time these men wasted moving from one job to the next, and getting into one another's way. At General Mo-

tors somebody had a bright idea—instead of sending the man to the work, why not bring the work to the man?

They began trying experiments; and very soon Henry's scouts told him about it. He couldn't afford to be left behind, so he tried it too. The work of assembling the flywheel magneto, a small but complex part, was put on a sliding table, just high enough to be convenient for the workers, who sat on stools, each performing one operation upon a line of magnetos which crept slowly by. In the old way, a man doing the work of making a magneto could turn out one every twenty minutes; now the work was cut into twenty-nine operations, performed by twenty-nine different men, and the time per magneto was thirteen minutes and ten seconds. It was a revolution.

They applied it to the making of a motor. Done by one man, it had taken nine hours and fifty-four minutes. When the assembling was divided among eighty-four different men, the time for a motor was cut by more than forty percent.

Early in 1913 this revolution hit Abner Shutt, subforeman of spindle-nut screwing. One sunshiny morning he was ordered out to "John R. Street," which runs through the Highland Park plant, to take part in an experiment in assembling a chassis, which is the car with its wheels before the body is put on. They had a platform on wheels, and a rope two hundred and fifty feet long, with a windlass to draw it. The materials to be used had been placed in piles along the route, and six assemblers were to travel with the platform and put a chassis together on the way, while men with stop-watches and notebooks kept record of every second it took them.

By the old method of building a car on one spot like a house, it had taken twelve hours and twenty-eight minutes of labor to assemble one chassis. By this new crude experiment they cut the time more than half. So very soon they set to work to rip out large sections of the plant and build them over. A moving platform was installed, and the various parts of the chassis came to it either on hooks hanging from chains, or on small motor-trucks travelling up the aisles. Presently they raised the line to waist-height, and before long they had two lines, one for tall men and one for short.

A far cry from the days when Abner Shutt had travelled to the shed and rolled in two wheels by hand, and sorted out right spindle-nuts from lefts and screwed them himself. Now he oversaw a group of men whose every motion had been calculated by engineers. The completed wheels, product of an assembly line of their own, came on rows of hooks, and descended to exactly the right height to be lifted off and slid onto the axle. The man who did this did nothing else; another man put on the spindle-nuts and started them by hand; still another finished the job with a wrench. Before the engineers got through with studying those operations, they had cut the time of assembling a chassis from twelve hours and twenty-eight minutes to one hour and thirty-three minutes.

Once this process was established, the irresistible tendency was to increase the speed of the "belt". Henry Ford might insist, as he continually did, that competition was wrong, and that he did not believe in it; but the fact was that he was competing at every moment of his life, and would continue to do so as long as he made motor-cars. In a hundred different plants scattered over the United States efforts were being made to beat him. In the long run, the successful ones would be those who contrived, by one method or another, to get the most out of a dollar's worth of labor. This was true from the first motion of the first hand which dug iron ore or collected the juice of rubber-plants in tropical jungles.

There was always a clamor from the sales department for more cars. When the plant was turning out a thousand a day, those who had the job in hand knew that by increasing the speed of the assembly line one minute in an hour, they would get sixteen more cars that day. Why not try it? A couple of weeks later, after the workers on the line had accustomed themselves to the faster motions, why not try it again?

Never had there been such a device for speeding up labor. You simply moved a switch, and a thousand men jumped more quickly. It was an invisible tax, like the tariff, which the consumer pays without being aware of it. The worker cannot hold a stop-watch, and count the number of cars which come to him in an hour. Even if he learns about it from the man who sets the speed of the belt—again it is like the tariff in that he can do nothing about it. If he is a weakling, there are a dozen strong men waiting outside to take his place. Shut your mouth and do what you're told!

## XX

All that was obvious, and no one knew it better than Henry Ford. It troubled his conscience, for he was an idealist, and believed in making people happy; he was also something of an economist, and in advance of the official economists he grasped the idea that if he paid men high wages, they would be able to buy Ford cars. Why should Henry worry about paying out money when he was sure of getting it all back —and meantime he would have the fun of making cars? More common sense!

Henry prepared a bombshell, and on the fifth of January, 1914, he threw it into the public arena. The Ford Motor Company was going to divide with its workers a bonus of ten million dollars every year, in a form which would bring to the lowest paid workers in the plant a minimum of five dollars per day. This bonus would take about half the profits which the company was expected to earn in the coming year. At the same time the working day, which had been nine hours, was reduced to eight.

The first effect of this announcement was to make the fame of Henry Ford. Up to that time his car had been known, but he himself had been just a manufacturer. Now, overnight, he became one of America's national heroes. A furious controversy arose— on the one side labor and the social up-lifters, on the other side manufacturers, business men, and the newspaper editors who voiced their point of view. The former said that Henry Ford was a great thinker, a statesman of industry; the latter said he was a self-advertiser, a man of unsound mind, a menace to the public welfare. Industry could not pay such wages, and anyone who said it could was leading the workers into a trap. "Distinctly Utopian and against all experience," said the solemn New York "Times", and they sent a man to Detroit to ask

Henry Ford: "Are you a Socialist?" Henry didn't know just what a Socialist was, but he felt safe in guessing that he wasn't one.

The next effect was that large numbers of the workers of America hopped the first freights to Highland Park. The company issued warnings, but it was too late. On the first day there were ten thousand in front of the gates, and by the end of the week, when the plan was to go into effect, there was an army. Streams of icy water were turned on them, and police reserves fought for two hours to drive them back from the gates. Stones were thrown and windows smashed—a painful end of a perfect day. The half-frozen workers went away with rage against Henry in their hearts; but those fortunate ones like Abner Shutt, who were inside, didn't lose much sleep about it. This was a hard world, and a fellow who had something had to hold onto it.

Mr. and Mrs. Ford travelled to New York, and discovered what it meant to be famous in America. A swarm of reporters met them at the railroad station, and the popping of flashlight bulbs made known that a hero had arrived. In the hotel the photographers broke down the potted palms in order to get a "shot" at him. There was a sack of mail waiting, and presently the telephone had to be disconnected on the floor which he occupied. Thus far in his life Henry had been a plain American citizen; but now he would be forced to live like a European potentate, with armed guards on duty, and a barrier of secretaries standing between him and the public which adored him and feared him all at once

—but in any case had to know what he thought about labor unions, prohibition, birth control, and the European situation; also what he ate for breakfast and what toothpaste he used afterwards.

All this news appeared in the Detroit papers, and the fourteen thousand employees who stood to get that minimum wage learned for the first time what a really great man their employer was. When he came back, they read all about his home life, which hitherto had been concealed from them. They read about his love of birds, and how he had fixed up houses for two thousand on his place; how he had refused to use the front door of his home for two weeks, because a pair of linnets had built a nest above it. "No matter what the weather is," said he, "the bobolinks always come back to Dearborn on May 2."

They saw pictures of him sitting in his library, or at his desk in the office, giving orders over the telephone for the making of a new world. They saw him at his winter sport of skating, and later on at his summer sport of pitching hay on the farm, along with his son, Edsel, now twenty-one years old. Also they saw pictures of him sitting in that first horseless carriage, which Abner Shutt had helped to lift out of a mudhole on Bagley Street. Mr. Ford had bought back that relic, and now kept it in a rear room of his office, and hauled it out now and then to prove that it would still run, and to have a picture taken, with himself at the steering-rudder, and Mrs. Ford in the other seat, or Thomas A. Edison, or John Burroughs, or some other of his friends.

## XXI

The public had got the idea that the Ford Motor Company was going to pay each of its men not less than five dollars a day; the men had got the same idea, and there was some dismay when it was discovered that this was not the program. The former wages were to remain unchanged; but every two weeks the men were to receive a bonus—provided they had "qualified." There was a catch in that word, and it was a complicated catch, which some of the men never did solve.

There were three groups. Married men had to be "living with and taking care of their families." Single men over twenty-two had to be "living wholesomely," and "of proved thrifty habits." Young men under twenty-two, and all women, had to be "the sole support of some next of kin." To ascertain these facts concerning fourteen thousand employees of a manufacturing company was no small task of research; to perform it, Henry Ford set up a Social Department of the Ford Motor Company, with a staff of fifty moral and properly certified young gentlemen to assist him. Two years later he persuaded an Episcopal clergyman, the dean of St. Paul's Cathedral in Detroit, to resign that honorable job and take charge of the morals of the Ford workers.

Henry and his new staff had agreed upon the elementary principles. They were going to break up the evil habit of the foreign workers' taking boarders into their homes, which made the home a money-making device and undoubtedly gave opportunity for promiscuity. They were going to compel unmarried men to visit a clergyman or a justice of the peace before they set up housekeeping. They were going to break up the habit of boys running away from home and failing to support their elderly relatives. They were going to stop at least the worst drinking, and see that homes were kept clean, and that children and sick people were taken care of. These were worthy aims, and the prize to the worker who would assist the Social Department was a check every fortnight amounting to somewhere between twenty-five and fifty dollars.

So far as the Shutt family was concerned, the problem was easy. Milly had her marriage certificate framed and hanging on the wall, and she had a bulge in her stocking where she habitually kept the money which Abner brought home on Saturday evenings. It was true that her home wasn't as spick and span as it might be, but that was not her fault, for she suffered from "falling pains", and had had a doctor to diagnose them. The young man who came to interview her about her affairs was kind and sympathetic, and gave her so much useful advice that Milly couldn't remember it all. She was told to use some of the extra money to have a strong woman come in to do scrubbing and cleaning once a week. She was told about the cuts of meat, and how the cheap ones could be made good by much boiling. She was told of the importance of plenty of green vegetables and some fresh fruit for the children.

Also they discussed the subject of rents, which were increasing rapidly in and about Highland Park; Milly said that she and Abner had had it as a dream of their life to own their home,

and readily agreed that a part of the bonus money would be used for that purpose. The man went away, and the facts which he had gleaned were entered in a vast card-catalog at the office of the Social Department, and Abner Shutt was informed that he had "qualified." In addition to his regular pay of forty-two cents per hour he would have a profit-rate of twenty-six and one-half cents an hour, which meant that every second Saturday he would receive an additional check for twenty-five dollars and forty-four cents.

It passed Abner's comprehension how any man or woman could fail to be grateful for such divine compassion on the part of Mr. Ford. But human nature is notoriously perverse, and many of the men grumbled bitterly against having their private lives investigated, and they changed the name of the new department from "Social" to "Snooping". Instead of complying loyally with the terms of the agreement, they set to work to circumvent it by diabolical schemes. The foreigners turned their boarders into brothers or brothers-in-law; the young men hid their girls for a while, or put them forth as orphan sisters; some evil ones even went so far as to hire an aged relative pro tem, in order to do their qualifying. Some of these tricks were caught up with, and the tricksters were fired, and there was not a little spying and tale-bearing and suspicion.

## XXII

The only fault the Shutt family had to find with the new arrangement was that prices began to increase so fast. First of all, the wicked landlords started raising rents. The Shutts had been paying twelve dollars a month, and now were told that the rent was twenty. They set up a howl, of course, but the agent said they could pay or quit.

Abner spent a Sunday afternoon riding around talking with other agents, and getting a lesson in elementary economics. Highland Park was going to be a more expensive place to live in, since the kind Mr. Ford was distributing ten million extra dollars every year. Why shouldn't the owners of lots and buildings have a share in all that prosperity? Just as it had occurred to Abner, so it occurred to many landlords, that it would be a nice thing to buy a Ford car, and take the family for an outing in the country on Sundays. Or maybe to go fishing on one of the Michigan lakes in summer, or to spend the winter in Florida—why not?

Abner and Milly decided to plunge and buy a home at once; whereupon they got another lesson in economics— the prices of homes had just about doubled since the Ford Motor Company's announcement. If only Abner could have bought before the announcement was made! If only he had had a tip! Some of Mr. Ford's associates had known, and hastened to buy land —and now they were "holding it" at such and such a high price, and making it nearly as hard for the Shutt family as if there hadn't been any bonus!

As time went on this cruel lesson was taught to them over and over. Milly, most careful of shoppers, took to keeping her family hungry and wore out her own tired legs, trying to find a store where she could buy food at the prices she had got used to in the old,

Before Bonus, era. There just was no such store, and the dealers hastened to explain that their own rents had gone up, and also wages. Who would work in Highland Park for the old wages, when he too had to pay higher rents and higher prices for food? There was something wrong with the world!

The one person who got exactly what he wanted out of that bonus was Henry Ford himself. In the first place he got the reputation of being America's Number One employer; no small advertising item for the Ford car, which was sold to the plain people, many of them workers, and others of them idealists like Henry. When they traded in the old flivver for a new one, they liked to feel that they were helping along a great philanthropic experiment. "Help the other fellow," said signs posted all over the plant, for visitors as well as workers to read.

Furthermore it meant that Henry got the pick of the labor of the country. He could investigate and be choosey, and when he hired a man he could keep him. The change in the labor turnover was extraordinary. In order to keep fourteen thousand men in the Before Bonus era, they had had to hire fifty-three thousand a year. But in the next year they hired only 6508, and most of these were new men, taken on because of the growth of the business.

## XXIII

A real estate agent got hold of Abner and Milly. Very solemnly he assured them that he had the last great bargain available in Highland Park. He was telling them for their good, not his own; if they let the opportunity pass, it would be snapped up by some one else and they would regret it all their lives. The house had six rooms, bigger than they had aspired to; but they felt so prosperous, and they knew that the youngsters would grow, and the little girl could not always sleep in the room with her parents. After much agony of soul they decided to take the risk.

They paid thirty-one hundred and fifty dollars for the house, which they could have got for a thousand dollars less in the Before Bonus days. They paid six hundred dollars down, which was practically everything they had been able to save in ten years, and they agreed to pay twenty dollars a month, plus interest, which at the beginning amounted to some thirteen dollars a month additional.

The taxes would be a surprise item —the agent had avoided mentioning them, and the family had never owned any property before. The interest would diminish, but they would be paying on the principal for the next eleven years. The agent argued that they would be paying rent in any case, and rents would be sure to go higher— in which, as it happened, the agent was right.

Everything was going up, for a strange and terrible reason. The nations of Europe, at least the greater number of them, chose this summer to plunge into war. Abner read about it in scare headlines across the top of his evening paper, a few days before he and his wife signed the contract for the house. Sitting on the front porch after supper, he read the news aloud to Milly. Every day some new nation toppled into the abyss; armies were marching, and presently they were fighting, and the headlines read,

"Twenty Thousand Germans Slain"— or maybe it would be Frenchmen or Russians or Austrians or Serbians. All of those nations were just names to Abner, and he had no idea what they were fighting about. He congratulated himself that he lived in a free country, where people had too much sense to behave in such a crazy fashion.

That was the reaction of most everybody he knew, including his employer. Mr. Henry Ford did not believe in war. He had expressed his opinion of it many times—along with his opinions on high tariffs, the gold standard, bankers, labor unions, and the Mexican situation. This war was the worst thing that had happened in modern times, and it all came because people thought they could get rich by seizing other people's wealth, instead of putting their brains to work to create wealth for themselves. If people were determined to fight, it was their own affair; but this much the president of the Ford Motor Company could say, and he said it with the utmost emphasis: his company would do no war work, and would sell nothing to any belligerent.

This he stated, and to the consternation of the warring powers, he meant it. Agents of the British government travelled to Highland Park to buy Ford cars, and they were told there were none for sale to them. They couldn't believe their ears, and explained that there must be a misunderstanding, they would pay cash; they were prepared to write checks on the long-established banking-house of J. P. Morgan and Company, located at the corner of Broad and Wall Streets in the city of New York. Yes, Mr. Ford had heard of that concern, but it didn't make any difference, he was selling no cars to be used in war.

Of course it may be that the British found some way to get hold of some, in spite of the stubbornness of one pacifist in business. It was far too much to expect that all the executives and salesmen of Ford cars should be shining idealists like their employer. The statement that money has no smell is as old as the ancient Romans, the best business men of their time. It could not be expected that Henry Ford would personally follow all the cars that were purchased from him, and make certain that none of them found their way to a country known as Canada, which lay just across a narrow river from Detroit. During the first year of the war Henry sold more than three hundred thousand cars, during the second year he sold more than half a million, and during the third year he sold more than three-quarters of a million. But the increase may have been because other motor-manufacturers, supplying the warring nations, left a larger share of the American market to Henry.

## XXIV

The Shutt family moved, and this time they meant it to be for life. Their new home sadly needed paint, and the picket-fence was on the verge of collapse, and the lot, fifty by one hundred and twenty, was full of weeds; but to them it seemed a mansion, and Abner would never be too tired when he came home to dig up a few feet of ground and plant onions and turnips. Milly got a woman to scrub and clean for two whole days, and the children caught the fever and insisted on trying to help. Mr. Ford was right, as

usual; it was a good thing to own your own home.

So far as the Shutt family was concerned, there could be no question that the benevolent bonus plan was a complete success. Abner and Milly used their money for exactly the purposes which Mr. Ford approved. The kind agent who represented his Social Department came and looked things over, and the little family was in a glow of gratitude to him, and to the godlike man who had solved so many problems of their lives and made such happiness for them.

The factory was working in two eight-hour shifts, which meant that Abner started at six in the morning and got home in the middle of the afternoon. That gave him plenty of time to make a garden and repair the fence to keep the neighbors' chickens out. In the fall he even got up the courage to give the house a coat of paint; it would pay in the long run, for it was theirs.

Also he had time to watch the children grow, and to teach them. Johnny was now ten years old, a serious and sturdy youngster, interested in everything his father did and said. He took his younger brothers and sister safely to school, and when he came home he helped his mother, and pulled the weeds out of the garden, and followed Abner about trying to have a hand in the work. He had a quick mind, and no one would doubt that he was going to get along.

The second boy, Henry Ford, was the one who made the problems. Hank, as the boys took to calling him, had no interest in sweeping the porch steps or pulling weeds. He resented every kind of restraint, and would not even let his older brother hold his hand when they were crossing the street. He thought of a fence as something to be climbed over, and he was always on the wrong side of it, breaking a window with a baseball, or getting into other mischief with the "gang." When his mother's scolding did no good, Abner would be called upon to "whale him"; and that wasn't entirely satisfactory, because it caused him to hide things from his parents and lie about what he had been doing.

Daisy was a sweet and gentle child, who already at the age of eight knew how to do housework and liked it. She was quite happy to sit on the front step and play with a rag-doll, talking to it devotedly. Presently she picked up a stray kitten, and after that the one care of her life was to keep the bad boys from teasing it. Abner fenced off a corner of the yard and got a few hens, and in the spring, when a brood of chicks was hatched, Daisy could hardly be torn away from the place.

A fascinating thing to see the minds of children unfolding. All four of these learned quickly, but they learned different things. Johnny, you could see, was going to be a mechanic like his father; the hope of his life was to be allowed to take off the wheels of the bicycle and clean and grease the bearings, and make the delicate adjustments putting them on again. The one who was going to manage men was little Tommy; in spite of being the youngest, he always wanted to tell the others what to do, and when he could not manage boys he managed girls. He was a pretty little fellow, eager and excitable, and with a keen sense of justice which was going to cause him a lot of trouble in the world.

## XXV

Time passed, and the Ford Motor Company continued to prosper, and Abner Shutt continued to receive his weekly wage, and his bonus every other Saturday. He made his payments on the house and fed his family, and was able to save a bit, in spite of prices continuing to creep up. The papers now said that it was on account of the war; the nations of Europe were sending over here and buying everything in sight.

Even so, an old dream began to stir in Abner's soul. His home was nearly three miles from the place where he worked, and there was no convenient street-car line, and in rain or snow it was no fun riding a bike, and working in half-damp clothing. Many of the men had got second-hand cars, and now rode to the plant in style, and sometimes picked up a few "jitney-nickels" carrying others. The families of these lucky ones got an outing on Sundays; they could go and see the old folks, or drive out into the country and buy vegetables and fruit and eggs at less than city prices. Why shouldn't the Shutt family enjoy such pleasures?

There had come to be a regular market for used cars, with a schedule of prices pretty well standardized, like everything Henry Ford had to do with, even indirectly. Fords didn't lose value so fast as other cars, because those who drove them were not so urgently in need of being fashionable. Henry had declared, over and over again, that there was no sense in changing a car just to have it different, and that the Ford Model T was going to remain a Ford Model T. And because he said it, it was so. But that did not change the fact that the American people liked to be up to date, and that the Ford agencies and salesmen liked to help them in this ambition. So it had come about that there had been a 1913 model of Model T, and now there was a 1914 model of Model T, and presently there would be a 1915 model of Model T. Those who could afford the luxury of being up to date, or who thought it was good advertising for their business, would hasten to trade in their old car and get a new one.

On one of the vacant lots where the used-car dealers did business, Abner found a 1910 Model T which was offered for "three hundred and a quarter"..If there was anything which Abner knew it was Ford cars; he had probably screwed on the spindle-nuts of this one with his own hands, and he tried it out and satisfied himself that with a little tinkering now and then, he would be able to drive it for the next ten years. In that time he would save quite a bit of carfare, to say nothing of knee and ankle-grease.

The family didn't take such a step without consulting the kind man of the Social Department. He came and talked it over with Milly, and agreed that it was a sound plan; also it was a way to compliment their employer, by keeping one of his cars upon the road. So Abner paid fifty dollars down, and signed an agreement to pay ten dollars a month thereafter, with interest at two percent a month, which was more than it sounded to be. If they didn't pay it, the car would be "repossessed"; but they meant to pay it.

Here came Abner with the royal coach, and the whole family streamed out to gaze at it. This was quite certainly the proudest moment of their

lives so far; their social position in the neighborhood rose immensely. One of Milly's brothers had a car and had taken her for a ride twice; but none of the kids had ever been in one of these creations which their father had been working on and talking about for the past eleven years. The four of them just filled the back seat, and they squealed and jumped and bounced up and down with delight. Abner had to take them all the way around the block before supper.

They had no garage to keep the car in. This was one more job Abner would do in his spare time, with the help of his old father, who had not forgotten that he was a carpenter, in spite of some eighteen years as a nightwatchman. Also it was something else to spend Abner's bonus money on. A hard thing to hold on to money in this free and easy-spending land!

## XXVI

If Abner and Milly had known more about economics, they would have spared themselves all worry about finances. For as long as the nations of Europe and Asia were continuing to make war, there would be an incessant demand for means of transport, and no lack of employment for those who could help to carry men and munitions to a battle-front. The world would continue to buy all the cars the Ford Motor Company could turn out; if Henry reduced the price of them, it would be because he foolishly chose to, and not because he had to.

The situation was understood by Henry Ford, and troubled his conscience not a little; for he was a sincere idealist, priding himself upon the fact that he had created a "clean" fortune, earned by producing useful things and not by robbing or oppressing anybody. But now he had the feeling that there were bloodstains on his money; the fact that the sales department wiped them off before turning the money over to him didn't fool Henry. He never let anybody fool him, and at this stage of his life he was not fooling himself.

He loathed war as a stupid, irrational, and altogether hideous thing. He began to give less and less of his time to planning new forges and presses, and more and more to writing, or at any rate having written, statements, interviews, and articles denouncing the war and demanding its end. To other business men, who believed in making all the money you could, and in whatever way you could, this propaganda seemed most unpatriotic; the more so as many of them were actively working to get America into the conflict, and multiply their fortunes overnight. The vice-president of the Ford Motor Company, James Couzens, who had put in a thousand dollars eleven years ago, now resigned his position, with a statement that he did not care to be carried along "on Henry Ford's kind of a kite."

But there were others who thought it was a grand kind of a kite; the pacifists, the social uplifters, all those men and women who thought there was something wrong with the world, and made it their business to find out what it was and how it could be changed. Such persons are generally without much money, not having time to think about it, nor the talent for taking things away from their fellows. But they are always on the lookout for some one who has the money, and may be persuaded to use it to carry out their ideas.

Ever since his bonus plan had been announced, Henry Ford had been the goal in life of half the "cranks" of America; a stream of them came every day to his office and his home, and the postman brought a sackful of letters from others. Henry did not see the visitors, and did not read the letters, nor did his secretaries answer them. But now that he had come out as a pacifist, many of these people got to talk with him, and the rumor spread that Henry Ford was keeping dangerous company, and being used by wicked and designing people. Such tales were readily believed by military-minded persons who were trying to get America to spend money on preparedness, and by socially prominent persons who took the manners and ideals of the British ruling classes as the noblest and finest on earth.

So Abner, reading his afternoon newspaper, became dimly aware that people were criticizing and sneering at his great and good employer. He was shocked, and as time went on he became indignant. Others might waver in their loyalty, but never Abner Shutt. He watched that great industry growing, he saw new structures arising, of whose purpose he had only a dim understanding; but he knew they were right, because Mr. Ford and his staff were directing them. Mr. Ford was one who built useful and sensible things, and it was wreckers and plunderers who hated him and wanted to down him. Abner hated war, but one war he would gladly have marched to, and that was a war of Henry Ford against Wall Street.

## XXVII

In Hungary had lived before the outbreak of the war a lady by the name of Rosika Schwimmer. She had been active for woman's rights, and the protection of children, and peace, and other honorable things. Pacifist agitators being not so welcome in the Austro-Hungarian Empire in wartime, Rosika moved to the neutral countries, and finally to the United States, where she co-operated with Jane Addams and others in a plan to organize "continuous mediation".

Rosika came to see Henry Ford, and won him to this plan. She also won him to Rosika. Here was a woman who really knew about peace and how to get it. She held before his eyes the hideous image of twenty thousand young men being slaughtered every day, and of men in high positions who looked upon this fact with cold, professional eyes, willing to have it continue indefinitely, upon the theory that their set of warring nations had a larger population, and could stand the drain upon "manpower" longer than their enemies.

Henry was given to making up his mind quickly. When he wanted something, he went after it. At Rosika's suggestion he called upon President Wilson, and made certain that no action displeasing to the British Empire was going to be taken from Washington. If it were to be done, Henry would have to do it himself. Rosika suggested the idea of taking a large delegation of American pacifists to visit the neutral countries, and there to work out a program for "a conference of neutral nations for continuous mediation among the belligerent nations."

Such a movement, once started, would grow rapidly.

Henry decided to charter a ship, and invite the pacifists of the United States to accompany him on a crusade. It was in November of 1915, and somebody suggested the slogan: "Get the boys out of the trenches by Christmas." That sounded good to Henry, and he adopted it. If it had been a contract for the making of a hundred thousand speedometers for Ford cars, he would have figured the processes involved, and known that it couldn't be done in that time. But here was a question of saving the lives of twenty thousand boys a day—a million more lives before Christmas—and Henry was in a hurry. It was, he said, "not a boast, but a prayer."

He selected a staff of his employees to run the affair, and hired a steamship, the "Oscar II". With the help of Rosika and his new pacifist friends, he selected a list of distinguished persons, including the governors of forty-eight states, and the Secretary of State, William Jennings Bryan. Mr. Bryan declined, and so did forty-seven governors, but many other persons volunteered to take their places, and out of the kindness of his heart Henry told them to come along. He was new at reforming the world, and really didn't know how many queer kinds of people there were running loose.

When Henry's announcement appeared, it was the greatest sensation since the outbreak of the war. America's most sudden millionaire was going to sail a "peace ship" across the stormy Atlantic, braving the submarines and bringing a cargo of pacifist agitators. Teddy Roosevelt, who felt extremely warlike, called it "the most discreditable thing in the country"; a Wall Street lawyer who had run against Teddy for President now called Henry Ford "a mountebank and clown." "Ford's folly," "a peace junket," "a jitney joyride," said the Wall Street newspapers. Said Henry: "The fight to stop the war is too big a thing to stop before the vaporings of editorial-writing comedians."

## XXVIII

The German militarists had been skillful at building a war-machine, but they had not been so good at understanding the minds of other people, and their diplomatic department had blundered badly, and got most of the civilized world at war with them. They might have been glad to have a chance to back out, and make a better start later on. But meanwhile the British navalists, who had been forced to watch an enemy fleet being built just outside their front dooryard, had no idea in the world of letting the war be ended until they had destroyed that fleet. That was what they had in mind, and they held to it with all the power and prestige of their empire—not only its cannon and its gold, but the eloquence of its literature, the piety of its moral code, the sanctity of its church, and the majestic self-sufficiency of its governing classes.

These forces had influence in New York; and there were native forces to supplement them. Wall Street was enjoying a boom the like of which had never been known in history. Everything that could be used in a world war was going up, and seventeen thousand new millionaires were being made in America. The old-established bank-

ing firm of J. P. Morgan & Co., at its old place of business at Broad and Wall, was handling billions of Allied dollars, supervising their distribution among the greedy "war-babies." All the Wall Street banks were stuffed with money, and the great New York newspapers and magazines, clients of these banks and some of them directly controlled, were keen for the continuing of the war and the destruction of the German fleet. Orders had gone forth to make a monkey of Henry Ford and a monkey-cage of his peace-ship, and the job was done with a thoroughness acquired by generations of training in cynicism and mendacity.

It was possible for an honest man in those days to realize the inadequacy of Henry Ford's mind for the task he had undertaken, and still to admire the courage and unselfishness he was displaying. It was possible for an honest man to believe that Henry Ford was mistaken, and that it was better for the war to be fought out and the Kaiser overthrown. But historians, looking back upon the events from the vantage-point of years, seeing what use the Allied diplomats made of their opportunity, seeing the ideas of truth and fair-dealing they cherished, the kind of peace they made and what came out of it—the historians would begin to ask whether Henry Ford and his "Ship of Fools" did not show more sense than all the chancelleries of Europe and the British Empire.

## XXIX

Abner Shutt would come home in the afternoon, and take off his shoes and put his stockinged feet before the kitchen stove, and read about the world and its doings. When he read that Mr. Ford was going to end the war, he was not surprised; on the contrary it seemed to him most proper and sensible. He had long ago decided that his employer was the greatest man in the world, and if now the crowned heads and potentates of Europe recognized the fact, it would be the best thing for them and their unhappy peoples. Mr. Ford would show them how to run things, and very soon all workingmen would be getting five forty-eight per day like Abner.

The sub-foreman of spindle-nut screwing read about the scenes at the sailing of the peace-ship; the big streamer upon it, reading, "Peace at any Price"; the famous ones who came, whether to sail or to bid goodbye to others; the crowds and the bands of music, the shouting and singing and making of speeches. Mr. Ford arrived in a big brown overcoat, fur-lined, with his friends, Bryan and Edison, to see him off. Some one presented Henry with an armful of roses, and standing at the rail he tossed these down to friends in the crowd. The band on the pier played "Tell the boys it's time to come home."

A theatrical man in a heavy ulster took a position on the upper deck, constituting himself master of ceremonies and bellowing forth introductions through a megaphone. "The fellow who makes light for you to see by. Ladies and gentlemen, please give three cheers for Thomas Alva Edison. Hip, hip, hooray. And now will the band please repeat that soul-stirring selection, 'I didn't raise my boy to be a soldier'."

Two of the peace pilgrims had arranged to be married on board, with Ford and Bryan as witnesses. There came a man with a new philosophy of religion, and a poet with a roll of manuscript addressed to the goddess of peace. There came vegetarians, prohibitionists, and the president of the Non-Smokers' League. There came a man with a cage containing a squirrel for Mr. Bryan. After the ship had started, a man leaped into the sea and tried to swim after it.

There were people on board that ship who had things of importance to say to the world. There was a judge who had spent his life establishing the first children's court; there was the first woman senator of the United States, and the first farmer-labor governor of a state. There was the widow of a manufacturer who had devoted his fortune to the single-tax, and a lovely young woman who had ridden a white horse down Fifth Avenue in America's first suffrage parade. But there was a pacifist clergyman from Chicago whose bountiful spread of white whiskers lent themselves to comedy effects; and there was a man who had once mounted a soapbox in Central Park and called upon the unemployed to follow him in a march to overthrow the government.

Mr. Ford himself went down with an attack of flu, and had to stay in his cabin, which is not so pleasant in mid-ocean and mid-winter. The news stories told about secret conferences in his cabin, and how everybody was clamoring to get his ear. They did not tell how the reporters burst into the cabin, demanding to talk to him, and giving as their reason the fact that they had been "scooped" on the death of the elder J. P. Morgan, and did not mean to be "scooped" on the possible death of Henry Ford!

## XXX

There were fifty-four news and magazine writers on the ship as Henry's guests. He believed in freedom of discussion, and in the rights of the people to know what was going on. A journalist of the London "Daily Mail" had presented himself, desiring to be taken as a guest, and failing in this, had bought a ticket as a second-cabin passenger. When the kind Mr. Ford heard about it, he invited the gentleman to join the party; being very naive, and having no idea who the journalist was, or what kind of paper he represented.

The owner of the London "Daily Mail" had risen in the same sudden and spectacular fashion as Henry Ford himself; only instead of selling honest machinery, he had been a merchant of sensations and scandals. He had made himself a multi-millionaire and a power, and since it was in Britain, he had got himself transformed from Alfred Harmsworth to Lord Northcliffe. His agent, taking advantage of a Michigan farm-boy, sent out over the uncensored wireless of the peace-ship detailed accounts of quarreling and fighting among the pacifists, and all kinds of ridiculous inventions about what was going on. These stories went to all the neutral nations; they were broadcast by the press of that greatest of all countries, the munitions empire, and told the world that Henry Ford was "a prisoner in his stateroom, tied to his bed by Dean Marquis and guarded by an armed gunman."

President Wilson had just sent to Congress a message calling for a heavy increase in the military and naval forces of the country; and of course that delighted Wall Street, and correspondingly exasperated the pacifists. At the sessions which went on all day and most of the night on the ship, the friends of Rosika Schwimmer brought in a resolution opposing Wilson's proposal, and declared that anyone who did not sign it would be put ashore at the next port.

There were a number of Americans who had been willing to leave their business and cross a stormy ocean in the cause of mediation, but who didn't consider that America should remain weak in the face of the submarine menace, and anyhow didn't care to have their country's policy dictated by a lady from Hungary. Vehement speeches on the subject provided copy for eager journalists, and made it easy to persuade the world that the "peace-ark" was a cat and dog fight.

When the vessel landed at Christiania, Henry Ford was shut up in a hotel room, guarded by secretaries and friends. His faithful Dean Marquis, the clergyman who had charge of the Social Department, had disapproved of this expedition, but had come along to help his employer. He now urged him to return home, and cablegrams from Henry's wife seconded the appeals. Presently it was announced that on account of ill health, Henry was taking the next steamer back, and would appoint committees to manage the affairs of the expedition, and a business manager to pay the bills.

The sorrowful pacifists went on and held their meetings, and did what they could to rally sentiment in the neutral countries. But the spotlight left them, following the "motor-magnate" home. When he arrived in New York, he declared that he was more of a pacifist than ever. He proceeded to publish full-page advertisements in two hundred and fifty newspapers, so full of attacks upon the munitions interests that the Navy League sued him for libel.

## XXXI

Henry Ford was back in Highland Park, attending to the completing of his second million of automobiles. Abner Shutt, who had never left Highland Park, went on overseeing his part of the assembly line; a job which might have seemed small to outsiders, but which provided Abner with plenty of cares. Labor was becoming scarcer, and more and more independent. Abner, as a sub-foreman, took the employer's point of view, and wondered how these lazy and shiftless fellows expected the company to keep going. Did they think that Mr. Ford was in business just to provide them with silk shirts and socks?

Abner had troubles at home also. His father was now in his sixties; for twenty years he had slept most of the day, and gone, seven nights of the week, to pace the corridors of the Desmond Car Company, a revolver in his pocket and an electric torch in his hand. Every few minutes he stopped and turned a key and pressed a button, to record the fact that he had not sat down to rest his tired old legs. But now these legs were giving out; Old Tom had become so crippled with rheumatism that he had to lie in bed, only getting up now and then to hobble a bit, groaning.

Tom Shutt had been working for this company some twenty-five years, but they turned him off without even

a word of thanks—just a printed notice in his pay envelope. He had a little money saved, but he and his old wife had no place to go, and Abner and Milly had to take them in. Abner was a dutiful son, and didn't mind, but it turned out a poor arrangement so far as concerned Milly and her children. The mother had become peevish, from years of pain and hard work; whereas the grandmother was gentle and kind, and presently the children were going to her for what they wanted, and that made Milly jealous. It was easy enough to win children by spoiling them, she said; and whatever the right and wrong of it, it was certainly a bad thing for a household to have divided authority. The second son, Hank, was now eleven, and beginning to display the uncontrolled nature which was to cause unhappiness to himself and his parents. When Milly in a rage took a strap to him, and then his grandmother cried over him and gave him candy, Milly appealed to Abner, and thereafter would hold the old woman to blame for all the troubles the boy caused them.

The father did what he could to keep the peace, and did not make things worse by worrying. That is not a wise practice for a workingman, who has so many uncertainties in his life, and troubles enough every day, without borrowing from the future. It was the nature of women to squabble, Abner had decided; and it was the nature of boys to have their wild period, but in the end to settle down and go to work. Abner's wages had been raised again, he was getting over six dollars and a half now, and that was enough to balance a lot of troubles in his opinion. He brought the money to his wife, knowing that she watched it closely; if it helped her to grumble and scold, well, Abner brought home honest weariness, and could sleep through any thunderstorm.

Prices were going up, and so were the demands of that growing family. So many things children wanted nowadays, that they hadn't dared to want in Abner's days! The boys all clamored for bicycles; and Abner told them to go to work in their spare time and earn the money. They were luckier than he had been, for they could go to school, and have food in the house when they got home. He told them what hard times had been like. Who could say when such times would come again?

They had one luxury, the family "bus". On Sundays and holidays Abner would drive them out to visit one of his brothers' families, or one of Milly's sisters. For years he had figured on buying farm products cheaply and bringing home a load each trip; but alas, so many people had cars now that the farmers had got wise, they put out stands by the roadside, and charged just about what the stores in town were charging. But you always had the hope of finding a bargain.

## XXXII

Tall chimneys continued to rise at the Highland Park plant, and to pour clouds of black smoke into the sky. Henry Ford was making steel, he was building new machinery, and new structures to house it. Sixteen hours a day he was rolling out lines of new flivvers, one of them every twenty-five seconds now. He was buying properties, branching out into one industry after another, to give him control of raw materials and means of making parts of his cars: steel, iron ore, coal, glass, rubber, cement—in order to make one flivver he needed a world.

Both Henry and Abner continued to read the news of the world, and to interpret it, each according to his understanding. Strange as it might seem, their minds moved together, undergoing the same changes at the same time. At the beginning of 1916, each had been firmly convinced that the war was a collective madness, and that the only good thing anyone could say was that the United States was out of it. But by the beginning of 1917 each was playing with such phrases as "freedom of the seas," and "national honor," and even "a war to end war."

It was a grim joke which the munitions empire and its bankers had played upon the pair of them. By the simple device of selling so much goods and lending so much money to the Allies, they had brought about a condition where the failure of these Allies to win the war would have brought the downfall of American industry. Nobody would have had a dollar to pay for an automobile. Henry would have had to shut down his plant, and Abner and his family would have starved.

The matter was not stated thus crudely in the American newspapers; but their tone and contents began to change to meet this situation. Whereas in 1916 Abner and Henry had read about the horrors of war, in 1917 they read about the horrors of submarine war. Also they began to read about the glories of French civilization, and the humane ideals for which the British ruling classes had always stood. So presently Abner Shutt began to say to all his fellows in the shop, "By Heck, them Huns ought to be put down!" And in February the pacifist Henry Ford was telling a New York "Times" reporter about a bright idea he had for a "one-man submarine", which he described as "a pill on a pole"—the pole being fastened in front of the submarine and the pill being a bomb.

Inspired by the eloquence of Woodrow Wilson, America at last plunged in to make the world safe for democracy. Abner Shutt redoubled his vigilance, seeing to it that no German spies did harm to the stream of flivvers which were now going to be freely furnished to the Allied nations—that is to say, exchanged for their bonds, which would later be repudiated. Abner was told all about the spy-danger in his evening paper, and how the Kaiser's agents were plotting to wreck American factories. This evil thing was called "sabotayge", and Abner was ready to give his life to prevent it. But, as it happened, no opportunity ever presented itself in the spindle-nut screwing department.

Henry also did his part. He continued to make cars, but sacrificed his customary increase in production, and instead made army trucks, caissons, ambulances, and half a million cylinders for "liberty motors", as the airplane engines were called. He made steel helmets, and listening devices, and experimented on armorplate for both ships and men. He made five thousand tractors, to be shipped to England and used to avert the threat of starvation caused by the submarine blockade. He bought a tract of land along the Rouge River, in the Detroit area, and put up a building a third of a mile long and a couple of blocks wide, where he started mass production of submarine destroyers, called "Eagleboats", a couple of hundred feet long, stamping the hulls entirely out of steel. Quite a racket in that place—and a worse one for the sailors who were caught out at sea in those products of a farmboy's dream.

### XXXIII

So for two years Abner Shutt had plenty of work, and his wages rose to eight dollars and a quarter per day, which seemed astronomical, but really wasn't so much, when skilled carpenters and bricklayers were getting eighteen, and the price of everything was going up as fast as wages. One real advantage the family got out of it—the payments on the house were fixed, and no landlord could raise them, as so many were doing to their tenants. Every time Abner stopped at the bank to make a payment, he chuckled to himself because money was so easy!

The sub-foreman rode in state to his work, and took a couple of fellows with him when the weather was bad, and they paid him a nickel each way. This was a hardship for the street car companies, and they tried to have a city ordinance passed to stop the practice—something which caused Abner Shutt and fellows like him to take an interest in politics. Another reason was that Mr. Ford ran for the United States Senate from Michigan, and there was a red-hot campaign, in which for the first and last time it was permitted to talk politics in the Ford plant. Henry's opponent was a naval officer, and the campaign was really a Navy League effort to punish a heretic. The opposition raised five million dollars and bought the state; Henry spent a lot of money too, but he spent still more collecting evidence of his opponent's spending, and later on had the satisfaction of seeing him brought into court and convicted of bribery.

Thanks to the efforts of Abner and Henry, America won the war; but for some reason the world wasn't yet entirely safe for democracy. There had come a new danger, a hitherto unheard-of kind of creatures called Bolsheviki. Many of them appeared in America, and they were even more dreaded than German spies. Abner was advised by the newspapers to keep a lookout for them, and he was ready to do his best, but the task was made difficult by the fact that they were always portrayed as having bushy black whiskers, and the only person he ever saw thus adorned was a Jewish peddler who came to the door one day and tried to lure Milly into buying laces and rayon stockings.

Of course there were grumblers in the shops; but there had always been such, and they looked just as they always had, that is to say, tired and overstrained workers; it was hard to realize that they were now in the pay of Moscow. People were restless, having been keyed to a high pitch by the war, and it had ended with disappointing suddenness, before they had a chance to perform the heroic deeds for which they had got ready. Abner saw men on street-corners, haranguing crowds; he chugged by in his flivver, never stopping, but now and then he would read how the police had arrested such men, and there had been riots.

## XXXIV

Henry Ford, who had done more than his share of the war work, came out to Southern California for a rest. He rented a modest house in a residence town called Altadena, where he and his wife and Edsel, now twenty-five years of age, spent a quiet winter.

There was an author living in that neighborhood who went to pay a call, and found the father and son in the garage, having set up a shop where they could tinker—as Henry had done in the old Bagley Street days before Edsel was born. In this place they had come upon part of an old carbureter, of a make unknown to them; and it was like Agassiz reconstructing the skeleton of a fossil creature from a fragment of bone. Henry and Edsel were fascinated by the problem of a certain aperture, the purpose of which they could not figure out. They showed it to the author and asked his opinion, but as it happened he was riding a bicycle, and did not know what a carbureter was.

This author was an idealist like Henry, dreaming of peace and human brotherhood. He saw violence in the world, and more in the future, and was seeking a way to avoid it, and persuade men to co-operate in making plenty and security for all. He hoped to convert Henry to his theories; and since Henry was lean and long of legs, they wandered for hours over the foothills of the Sierra Madre, looking up at snow-covered peaks and down into valleys green with orange groves, discussing the way to adjust the carbureter of the world.

Henry Ford was now fifty-five; slender, grey-haired, with sensitive features and quick, nervous manner. His long, thin hands were never still, but always playing with something. He was a kind man, unassuming, not changed by his great success. Having had less than a grammar-school education, his speech was full of the peculiarities of the plain folk of the middle west. He had never learned to deal with theories, and when confronted with one, he would scuttle back to the facts like a rabbit to its hole. What he knew, he had learned by experience, and if he learned more, it would be in the same manner.

The author asked him what he thought about the profit-system, and Henry looked puzzled. "What is that?" The other found this the strangest of questions. The biggest profit-master in America didn't know that the profit-system existed! It was M. Jourdain, in Moliere's play, excited to discover that he had been talking prose all his life! When it was explained to Henry, he insisted that you had to have profits. Who would work without them? Why should anyone do so?

In the minds of men who are not used to abstract thinking, there can exist side by side all kinds of contradictions. Only a little while after insisting that nobody could or would or should work without profits, Henry Ford began telling how, on the night that diplomatic relations were broken with Germany, he had been dining at the home of the Secretary of the Navy, along with the President and Mrs. Wilson, and had stated to them that it was his intention to turn over his plant and all its resources to the government without profits.

When the author pointed out this inconsistency, Henry exclaimed: "Ah, but that was in war!"

"But," said the other, "why not have public service in time of peace? Why not the same enthusiasm for feeding and clothing men as for killing them?"

Henry was willing to admit that engineers and inventors did their work for the love of it. They were not the money-making type. The same might be true of poets and such—Henry didn't know them so well. What he himself wanted with money was to do things. If society would provide him with the opportunity to direct great undertakings, he would be content. But when the author suggested that the people might own the automobile industry and put Henry in charge of it, he struck a snag in the industrialist's mind. Henry didn't want any politicians butting in on his work. He was ready with instances of graft, incompetence, and favoritism: things which did not exist in the Ford plant.

He cited the railroads. They had broken down during the war, and the government had had to run them. They needed a complete job of reorganization, and Henry had talked to the Secretary of the Treasury, who had the matter in hand, and had been invited to submit proposals and figures. Henry had done so, at some trouble and expense, but nothing had been done about it. The Secretary of the Treasury was a Wall Street man, he believed in the Wall Street banks and served them, and could not really serve the public interest.

"That is exactly the point," agreed the other. "It is private interest which paralyzes politics, and makes graft, buying public servants to its own ends."

But that was too great a leap of the

mind for Henry Ford. Graft to him was the very nature of politics; also waste and incompetence. He insisted that he could run the postoffice as a private enterprise, better than the government was running it. He would not even admit that the Altadena fire-department was a thing to be publicly owned. Let some competent business man attend to putting out fires.

The author told how he had groped his way through these problems. As a youth, reading history, he had observed that monarchy was an excellent thing when you happened to have a good king; the trouble began when you got a bad one, and had no way to change him. That was why the king business had broken down in the end; and the industrial king business was breaking down because there were so few Henry Fords. The listener's modesty did not permit him to accept that argument; but he admitted it indirectly a little later, when he said that the reason there were no unions in the Ford shops was because the men didn't want them. If they wanted them, they could have them.

One of Henry's severest critics had been Theodore Roosevelt; and Henry was startled to hear the author say that they had the same kind of minds. "I have talked with him, Mr. Ford, and had to give up the effort to make him see an economic force or a social system. He sees individuals, good or bad. He saw malefactors of great wealth, committing crimes in Wall Street, and he made war on them; but it was a war of words, because he didn't know what to do. Now he has got his attention centered on foreign enemies, and wants to wield the big stick in Europe; which means that for the rest of his life he will play with the reactionaries. Watch out that this doesn't happen in your life, Mr. Ford."

## XXXV

In this land of sunshine and orange blossoms lived another American industrialist, not so rich as Henry Ford, but almost as well known, because his picture adorned every package of razor-blades which anybody purchased in those days. He too was a dreamer of brotherhood and peace. He had worked out in detail a plan whereby the business masters of America might make the change from private anarchy to public order without destruction and waste. They were to form a gigantic "People's Corporation," which would use the people's money to purchase the stocks of all going industries and operate them in the public interest.

King C. Gillette was now old, and could not undertake this task, but it was his dream to find some business leader who would take it up. He wanted to talk with Henry Ford, and they met in the author's home, and for two hours sat in front of the fire-place exchanging ideas. It was like the meeting of two billiard balls; there would be a sharp click, and they would fly apart, having taken no particle of substance, shape, or color from each other.

Henry Ford remained the super-individualist, who would have liked to turn the public schools over to private ownership. He was certain that sooner or later everybody would realize the wisdom of his method of turning out the best possible goods and selling them at the lowest possible price, and that if this were done, it would bring plenty and security to all. Nobody could persuade him that the automobile, a new device enjoying worldwide expansion, represented a special case in the industrial world. He was doing the same thing in steel, cement, rubber, glass, any number of lines of production, and insisted that he could make them for the general market, and pay everybody six or seven dollars a day.

King C. Gillette, a large, stout man, corresponded exactly to the cartoonist's idea of a plutocrat; but within that bulky body was the tenderness of a woman and the timidity of a child. He could not bear the thought of others' suffering, and he shrank from the clash of opinion and the anger of the world. He lived, withdrawn into his mind, a social analyst, tracing the capitalist process from its primitive beginnings, through its modern welter of confusion, to its inevitable and awful collapse. For thirty or forty years he had been making notes of the infinite varieties of capitalist waste; there were so many that he had a special secretary to type out his notes and to keep his lead-pencils sharpened so that he could make more.

The "Razor King" spent an hour or so presenting to the mind of the "Flivver King" the madness of the competitive system; goods created blindly, with every producer doing his best to hide from others what he was doing, and to deceive the public as to the real nature of his product. And for every instance of wholesale suffering thereby produced, the "Flivver King" had an answer which presently became a formula; it was "educational". "People will learn from it, Mr. Gillette."

"Yes, Mr. Ford, but what will they learn? It is not enough to say 'educational'. That means teaching, and be-

fore you teach you have to decide what you believe."

"People will find out for themselves, Mr. Gillette."

"But why shouldn't you and I find out for ourselves? You say we learn from our mistakes. For example, what did we learn from the world war?"

After some hesitation, Henry Ford was willing to say that the world war served to teach people the need of a league of nations.

"A political organization of governments. But don't you see that so long as the governments represent groups of economic interests, competing for raw materials and markets, they are bound to combine and play power politics, the very thing that got us into the war?"

Henry couldn't see that; or if he did see it, he couldn't admit it, even to himself. What would become of all his plans to open up new land, develop new processes, utilize new water power, increase production, improve products—if he had to admit that the more you do these things under the profit system, the more quickly you bring on over-production and throw millions out of work?

Some "New Thought" person had got hold of Henry's mind, and his belief in the profit system had become touched with mysticism. He had read Jack London's "Star Rover", and had taken up the idea of reincarnation. "We are living in the Eternal all the time," he declared. Gillette was willing for anybody to live in the Eternal, but why use that idea to confuse thinking on the subject of producing and distributing material goods. At the end of the futile conference the "Razor King" said to the "Flivver King": "In your own plant, Mr. Ford, you have order, you tolerate no waste. But in the outside world you have chaos and anarchy, and you defend it, and call your defense 'optimism'!"

## XXXVI

Henry went back to Detroit in the spring. He had several matters claiming his attention, among them two important lawsuits.

During the bitter days of 1916, when it had looked as if the United States was going to war with Mexico, Henry Ford had announced that any of his workers who joined the national guard would lose their positions. For this the Chicago "Tribune" had called him an anarchist; and Henry had flown into a rage and brought suit for a million dollars on grounds of libel.

Now as a matter of fact Henry didn't know very clearly just what an anarchist was; for that matter neither did the Chicago "Tribune" nor the people who read it. The best example one could find of a practicing anarchist had been Jesus Christ, but the "Tribune" readers would have wished to lynch anyone who told them that. To them the word anarchist meant a dangerous and lawless man; and about the most perfect illustration they could have found in their vicinity was the publisher of the Chicago "Tribune", which called itself the "World's Greatest Newspaper," and tried its best to be America's most vicious and hateful one.

The trial took place in the courthouse in the little town of Mt. Clemens, Michigan, and was another circus like the peace-ship, with Texas Rangers and other patriots as witnesses; swarms of reporters, and the whole world attending by proxy. A libel suit is a general inquiry into the life-history and the moral and intellectual totality of the man who brings it, and poor Henry had an uncomfortable time for two or three months. One of the world's greatest research departments had been working for three years to find out every absurd and mistaken thing he had ever said or done in his life, and now the shrewdest lawyers who could be hired were going to cross-question and expose him.

They picked out books with long words in them, and planned to ask Henry to read these, and so make him silly. Henry met that by the simple device of leaving his spectacles at home. People might assume that he didn't know how to read, but Henry said they were at liberty to assume anything they pleased. The fact was that he could read, but slowly, and he didn't know how to pronounce long words.

There were many more things he didn't know; for example, when the lawyers asked him about Benedict Arnold, he said he was a writer. The English-speaking world whooped with glee over this; it gave millions of smart people with book-learning an opportunity to feel superior to a multimillionaire. But the average American, who bought Henry's cars and drove them, was far more concerned to have him solve the problem of an efficient self-starter for his engine, than to have him know all about American history and English fiction. "I could find a man in five minutes who could tell me all about that," said Henry, and most of his customers thought that was a sensible answer.

Henry won his suit; that is to say, the jury decided that he was not an anarchist. But they didn't think he needed a million dollars, so they awarded him six cents. Henry went back to his home a wiser man in several respects; he not only knew the difference between Benedict Arnold and Arnold Bennett, but he knew the futility of libel suits, and thereafter the newspapers might lie about him all they pleased, and he would go on making automobiles.

## XXXVII

Henry had another and more important suit on his hands; one brought against him by the Dodge Brothers, those two machine-shop owners who had acquired Ford Company stock by making six hundred and fifty engines used in the first Ford cars. These brothers shortly afterward had started making a car of their own, and now had a big company. They still had their Ford stock; but what good did it do them, when Henry never paid any dividends?

Henry had peculiar notions on the subject. He didn't believe in paying rent for the use of money, and he had never in his life borrowed anything from bankers. He didn't believe in letting people get money which they hadn't earned by useful labor; so for sixteen years he had been taking the profits earned by the company and putting them into new land, buildings, machinery, and other means of making cars. That was fine for Henry, but it wasn't so fine for the Dodge brothers; they wanted the money to make Dodge cars, whereas Henry was using it to make Ford cars!

The Dodge brothers got a judge to issue an injunction forbidding Henry to spend any more money for extensions until he had paid dividends to his stockholders. The matter was tried out at law, and the Dodge brothers won, which very nearly broke Henry's heart. He gave out a story that he and Edsel were going to start a new company and make a new car to sell for two hundred and fifty dollars; thereby so frightening the minority stockholders that they sold out for a small part of the market value of their holdings. Even so, it was a thousand times what they had invested in the business. That James Couzens who had been a clerk in a coal-office, and had put in his savings, came out with thirty-seven million dollars, and used it to make himself United States senator from Michigan, the job which Henry had failed to get. Since he was an intelligent and open-minded man he made a very good senator, which Henry might very possibly not have done.

The newspapers faithfully reported these financial transactions, and Abner read the items aloud to old Tom. They went back in their memories to that day when they had gone together, Abner a little boy, to watch Mr. Ford trying out his steering-rudder in front of the Bagley Street shed. It had become the proudest memory of their lives, the one they talked about most frequently to everybody they knew. If only they had realized the future locked up in that baby-carriage with an engine; if only they had hitched their wagon to Henry Ford's car! They figured up how much money they had had in the savings bank in those days; if they had invested it in the stock of the Ford Motor Company, how much they would have now!

Everybody who had known Henry in those days did the same figuring. Millions of Americans did it, for no better reason than that they lived in Detroit, or had owned one of the early Fords, or had expressed belief in the future of the motor-car. It was the romance of America, the thing that lent glamor to people's lives, relieving the drabness of the work-a-day world. Business was like marriage, a lottery. The fact that such prizes were being drawn lent a thrill to being alive. Millions of men and women read the story of the Ford fortune, the Dodge fortune, the Couzens fortune, and brought themselves to a state of mind where they were ready to gamble on whatever came along. So the sellers of fake mining-stocks and oil-stocks and a thousand other get-rich-quick schemes found it possible to take hundreds of millions of dollars out of their pockets every year.

But you wouldn't hear much about that from the "Flivver King". That was the kind of talk one got from the "Razor King!"

### XXXVIII

John Crock Shutt, Abner's oldest son, was now fifteen; a big, round-faced boy with bright blue eyes, a nose like his mother's, slightly turned up, and hair that wouldn't stay in place. He was in high school, learning everything he could about metals and machinery. There now befell him a bit of good fortune which determined the rest of his life.

A year or so before America entered the war, Henry Ford had started a trade school, for the purpose of helping boys who had to leave school early, and turning them into well trained workers, of whom he had a constant need. It was Henry's own kind of school; the boys studied from books, but also they learned real work, producing things in various parts of the Ford shops and receiving thirty-five cents an hour, more than they could earn if they left school.

To qualify for that institution had been Johnny Shutt's goal in life from the day he heard about it. He made application, not failing to state that his father had been an employee of the Ford Motor Company from the first year of its existence. He was interviewed, his school record was examined, and he was accepted. He was so happy that he could not contain himself; thereafter he would come home each day and tell his mother and father all the wonders he had seen and done. He was going right ahead to learn everything about the making of an automobile, and the great Ford organization was going to be his world.

Thus one boy's problem was solved; but alas, no such fortune for the next one. Too bad that Johnny hadn't been the one to be named Henry Ford —it would have helped him in his career. Hank, the second boy, was what the school people called a "problem child"; one of his eyes had a squint, which gave him a sinister appearance, and maybe that was the reason he couldn't get along with people. Anyhow he lied to his teachers, and even to his fellow-pupils, so that they didn't like him. He played hookey from school, and when his father "lammed" him, he ran away and didn't come home. Prodded by the women-folk, Abner went to the police to try to find him, but perhaps they didn't work very hard, anyhow Hank wasn't found; he came back when he got good and ready, and Abner wasn't allowed to lam him again, because he threatened to disappear for good.

After that he cut school whenever he felt inclined; he took to disappearing at night—and presently it transpired what he was up to, he was one of a gang of boys breaking into freight-cars and carrying off goods. The police caught him, and there he was behind bars, his mother weeping to break her heart, unable to touch him, because there was an iron mesh between them. Such a dreadful disgrace to his honest and hard-working parents, who had taken their children to church every Sunday morning since they were able to walk. For some reason which Abner and Milly were powerless to fathom, it hadn't worked with one of the four.

Abner had to get half a day off from his job and go to court, taking the Rev. Orgut, his pastor, to prove that he was a respectable man. They pleaded with the judge, and Hank Shutt got what was called "probation", having to report to a court officer once a month and give an account of what he was doing. He was cowed for a while, and went to school, but would never again be happy in that family or with the church crowd. He had got himself marked, a young criminal; people would look askance at him, and he would reply with ridicule of their dull piety. A tough young guy; but, as it turned out, there was a way of life for that sort too.

## XXXIX

Henry Ford went on expanding his business. There was nobody to stop him now, he was master of his own house. He and his wife and son were the three directors of the Ford Motor Company; also they were the sole stockholders. There was a house-cleaning, and those who did not see eye to eye with the master got out. The war had done something to Henry, it had taught him a new way to deal with his fellow men. No more crusades, no more peace-ships, no more idealists getting hold of him and wasting his time! From now on he was a business man, and held a tight rein on everything. This industry was his, he had made it himself, and what he wanted of the men he hired was that they should do exactly what he told them.

He became more abrupt in his manner, more harsh in his speech. "Gratitude?" he would say. "There's no gratitude in business. Men work for money." On that basis he turned out of his organization many of his most faithful executives, men who had worked for him since the beginning. Sometimes he did not trouble to notify them, but let them come in the morning and find some one else installed at their desks. Now and then he would fly into an uncontrollable rage, and when the offending man reached his office he found that somebody had been there and smashed his desk to pieces with an axe. The man had no redress, for the desk had been "his" only in a way of speaking; like everything else, it was Henry's desk, and if Henry chose to smash it, or tell somebody else to smash it, why not?

Among those who took their departure was the Episcopal clergyman who had been in charge of the Social Department. Dean Marquis had been a wise counsellor during the five years he was in Henry's employ. But now in several cases he saw injustice done, and tried to intervene, and discovered that Henry was pretending not to know anything about actions which had been taken upon his express orders; he promised to investigate, but did nothing; and so, reluctantly, Dean Marquis realized that the period of idealism was past, and that there was no longer any place for a Christian gentleman in the Ford business machine. When he resigned, Henry dropped the attempt to decide how his employees should spend their money. He had been criticized for it, and now he said all right, let them have their own way. He was tired of having around him the reformers and idealists who reminded him of that stage of his career.

He was tired also of the promises he had made in those exalted days, and which he no longer wanted to keep. He had told President Wilson that he would return to the government every dollar of war profits he might make; he had published the same statement, with a flourish. He had made twenty-nine millions, and now found that he liked them. He liked the glory also, and allowed one of his biographers, a friend of his wife, to say that he had returned the money to the government. But the Secretary of the Treasury said that there was no record of such payment ever having been made.

## XL

The war had caused the destruction of hundreds of billions of dollars of wealth, and according to Henry's economics, that wealth had to be replaced; so a great business boom was certain. In the first year after the armistice the sales of the Ford car nearly doubled, and he felt that his theories had been vindicated. But in the middle of 1920 came a panic in Wall Street, and business went into a tailspin, and even the sales of Ford cars began to drop. Henry decided that prices had been forced too high by speculation, so he cut the price of his car from $525 to $440, far below the cost of production; he could do it, because he was using materials on hand.

He had been making a hundred thousand cars a month, and he kept it up. But the sales went on declining, until at last Henry realized that he was in a bad jam. In buying the Dodge and Couzens stock, he and Edsel had signed notes for seventy million dollars —and nearly half this amount was coming due, also eighteen millions of income tax to be paid to the government. These facts were known, and rumors began to spread that the company was trying to borrow money and failing. It is a peculiarity of our banking system to which Henry had often called attention, that the time a business man needs money is the time he cannot get it.

Stories appeared in the financial sections of the paper, which Abner did not read; then they broke into the news parts, where he saw them. A group of New York bankers had sent representatives to work out a plan for financing Henry Ford, the essence of the plan being that the financiers were to appoint a treasurer and handle the funds. Wall Street was going to take over the biggest independent manufacturer in the United States, who couldn't raise cash to the amount of one-tenth the value of his properties!

Abner read this story with bewilderment. He couldn't doubt that it was true—wasn't it there before his eyes? He talked about it with his shopmates; the younger ones said what the hell, they would get jobs somewhere, all jobs were alike. The older ones had a sense of loyalty, and were grieved. But there was nothing they could do. They went on making cars, wondering if the plant was going to shut down, and how soon.

Henry Ford read the stories too, but kept his own counsel, and went on making cars, even though everybody said he was crazy. He had a plan, and in due course the world would learn about it. All over the country were Ford dealers, more than seven thousand of them; they had the agencies, a valuable concession, in which many of them had invested all they owned. Now times were terrible, but prosperity would come back, and then they could be glad they had held on.

Early in December Henry sprang his coup. He had accumulated a great stock of cars in all the thirty-five assembly-plants which the Ford Motor Company owned in various parts of the country, and he now sent a letter to his agents, informing them that they were to take these cars immediately, each an assigned quota, paying cash. Telegrams of protest came back by the thousands. Impossible, declared the agents, it would mean ruin. But Henry was adamant; any dealer who did not take his quota would forfeit the agency.

Henry would not borrow from bankers—oh, no! He would put that painful job off on the dealers, the little fellows, each in his home town! Each would scurry round, argue and plead with his local banker, borrow from his friends, put a mortgage on his home;

somehow he would raise the cash and send it to Henry. Hadn't Henry created the car, and the business by which the dealer lived? What good would it do him to have the Ford agency, if there were no more Fords? Put up *and* shut up!

## XLI

Having loaded up the market with an oversupply of cars, the Flivver King now closed down his plant; a fine Christmas present for his men. It was a "reorganization", they were told; a long word, and many were not sure what it meant. The notice said it would be only a couple of weeks, but they didn't know whether to believe that. The notice said they would get the January bonus the first of the year; but again they weren't sure.

It was "hard times". Abner had told his children about it, and now he could say, "I told you so." He had saved a little money, fighting all the time to keep from spending it, being called a "tight-wad" and such names. Now he had to draw money from the savings-bank, and to both Abner and his wife it was like dying. He had meant to make repairs on the house, but didn't dare buy materials, and he hadn't the heart to work. Suppose they were to lose the house, on which they were only half way through paying!

Abner sat at home and brooded; or strolled down the street to talk things over with the neighbors—all Ford men, and all at home, waiting. A snowstorm made some work for a time, cleaning sidewalks; different work from what they had done on the assembly line, it made them puff. Abner had put on weight, which he took for a sign of health, but he was mistaken, for most of it hung around his belly. His legs had grown heavy, and varicosed from long standing. One thing a boss of the line could never do was to sit down; many workers could never stand up.

He tried to teach his fears to the children, but that wasn't easy. They were young, and so sure of themselves, ignorant of the world. Pretty little Daisy had her heart set on studying in a business college; she would be a fine lady stenographer, with plenty of silk stockings. Little Tommy, now eleven, was going to manage the world; already he was practicing in school, where they had all sorts of "activities". Always some place to hurry off to, no time to do chores at home, or even to get acquainted with their parents.

The waiting period stretched out to six weeks. Then, just as Abner was about to give up hope, the postman brought a notice to him to come back. He found out what his employer had been up to in the meantime; cleaning out all the remains of the war-work, planning a new industry, pared to the bone. Not a department, not a single employee that was not essential to the making of cars! No more statistics, no more welfare-work, no more frills and fads. Sixty per cent of the telephone extensions had been taken out. Young ladies who had been wearing silk stockings in the office now went to work on the magneto assembly lines.

They had been employing fifteen men per car per day. Now they had cut it to nine. In his public statements Henry said: "This did not mean that six out of fifteen men lost their jobs. They only ceased being unproductive." If that statement had

been true, the plant would have increased the production of cars by sixty-six per cent; but as a matter of fact they turned out just what they had been doing before the "reorganization," four thousand cars a day. They cut the overhead from $146 per car to $93, a saving of sixty millions a year. As a result, thousands of men took their places on the breadlines of Detroit and neighboring towns; and Henry went on publishing articles in the "Saturday Evening Post", proving that the machine process didn't cause unemployment.

Abner Shutt had been watching the work of five men, but now one foreman watched the work of twenty men —and Abner was one of the twenty. They put him back on the line. "We make no attempt to coddle the people who work with us," wrote Henry; so nobody apologized to Abner for his loss of status. "Men work for money," said the master; and Abner got the minimum of six dollars a day, and was grateful as a dog for his dinner.

Under this new deal the chassis came to him with the spindle-nuts already screwed on; it was Abner's job to put in a cotter-pin and spread it. The next man wielded a scoop, pasting a gob of brown grease into the cavity; by the time he had smoothed it level, the chassis had moved on to another, who screwed on the hubcap. Abner's job rested his tired legs, but his back began to ache abominably, and his arms were ready to give out from being held up in front of him continually. But he hung on like death and taxes, for he was over forty, the dangerous age for workers in any factory. "We expect the men to do what they are told," wrote Henry.

## XLII

In Dearborn, where Henry Ford had his office, there had existed a broken-down little weekly paper, the "Independent," with seven hundred subscribers. To help somebody out of a hole, Henry had bought it for twelve hundred dollars; and then, unable to let anything be wasted, he appointed an editor and told him how to put the paper on its feet. Himself always bubbling over with ideas, Henry gave the editor some "notes", which the editor proceeded to put into shape and publish as "Henry Ford's Page". By requiring all the agents to take a quota of subscriptions, the circulation of the "Dearborn Independent" was increased to a hundred and fifty thousand.

The author out in California had been at work upon a book exposing the dishonesty of the American press, and a good part of his talks with the motor-man had dealt with that subject. It was the only part which seemed to impress Henry; for he too had had experiences with newspapers, and was ready to agree that the country needed a journal which would speak for the people's welfare, and have the courage to give them the truth about what was going on. Henry had promised the author to fill that need in American life; he would make the "Dearborn Independent" a national organ with a circulation of two or three million.

The paper gave support to President Wilson in his efforts for a just peace and a League of Nations. But gradually it became clear to Henry that things were not working out as he had hoped. The world seemed to be on the verge of chaos. It was evident that there was some evil force at work, thwarting good capitalists like himself, who wanted to produce automobiles cheaply, and pay the workers high wages, so that they could buy automobiles and ride to their work of making more automobiles. Something desperately wrong; and Henry Ford sought earnestly to find out what it was.

Among those who managed to get by the secretaries was a Russian by the name of Boris Brasol, investigator of the wicked forces which were seeking to wreck Europe. They had already succeeded in Brasol's country, and had grabbed power in Hungary, and were close to it in Germany. The Bolsheviki? Ah, yes; but who was behind the Bolsheviki? Henry could understand that question, for as a successful business man, he understood that whenever anything happens on a big scale, there is always money behind it. It had been so in politics, it had been so in the world war, and no doubt was so in the world revolution.

The former agent of the "Black Hundreds" had the documents, carefully assembled, neatly typed, and indexed for ready reference. He was prepared to prove to any open-minded man that the troubles in the world today were due to a conspiracy of the Jews, an egotistical and evil-minded race which was plotting to seize the mastery of the world.

Just look, Mr. Ford! The bankers have been trying to take your business away from you. Who are they? Jews! All the international bankers are Jews: Rothschilds and Samuels and Barings, Belmonts and Baruchs and Strausses, Warburgs and Kuhns and Loebs and Kahns and Schiffs. The list of munitions magnates who made the war reads like the membership of a synagog. And look at the list of revolutionists: Trotsky and Radek and Zinovieff, Bela Kun and Liebknecht and Luxemburg. Does it surprise you that the Jews should be using strikes and revolutions to break the nations to their will?

Look, Mr. Ford! Here are proofs which would be valid in any court of law. We have the original documents in a safe place of deposit: the very words of the conspirators themselves, The Protocols of the Learned Elders of Zion. Henry read them, and it seemed to him that the very name was enough. Protocols! Who could make up a thing like that? What was a protocol?

## XLIII

Henry Ford started publishing in his "Dearborn Independent" a series of articles on The International Jew. He gave the Protocols of the Learned Elders of Zion to a startled America; he told the country all about the Jewish World Program, "the most comprehensive program for world subjugation that has ever come to public knowledge." Jewish leadership, operating in secret, was trying to destroy Gentile civilization. All the world's troubles, wars, strikes, insurrections, revolutions, crime, drunkenness, epidemics, and disasters were the work of organized malignant, corrupting Jews.

The paper kept this up for twenty consecutive weeks. It said: "The statements offered in this series are never made without the strictest and fullest proof." The American people, who knew Henry Ford for an honest and good man, were advised to take his word for the truth of every detail.

Some of the Jews in America pro-

tested, and even attempted to answer these articles. So Henry, who never did anything by halves, set to work to get the facts about the American Jews and what they were doing. He moved the greater part of his spy department from Dearborn to New York. He published a series on "Jewish Activities in the United States"; then another on "Jewish Influences in American Life"; then another on "Aspects of Jewish Power in the United States." He showed how Jews, controlling stage and screen, were depraving American morals; they were doing this, not because it paid, but as a deliberate plot to break down American civilization. Drunkenness was spreading, and it was not because the Jews were making money out of liquor, but because they wanted America drunk. Jews controlled the clothing trade, and so American girls were wearing short skirts. Jews controlled music, and so the American people listened to jazz and danced themselves crazy. The white slave traffic, the rise in rents, the move from the farms to the crowded cities, the spread of Bolshevism and of the theory of evolution, all were parts of the Jewish plot against the Gentile world.

Henry kept up this crusade for nearly three years. After the articles had appeared in the paper, they were reprinted in pamphlet form, five volumes, each containing two hundred and fifty closely printed pages, at twenty-five cents per copy, an achievement of mass production. Rural America, and plain native America in the towns and cities, subscribed to the "Dearborn Independent", and purchased these pamphlets, and studied them and quoted them as if they were Scripture.

Henry had said that "History is

bunk"; but of course he hadn't meant history such as The Protocols of the Learned Elders of Zion. Or the story of Benedict Arnold and his "Jewish aid" who was quartermaster to the American army and led the unfortunate young officer to his doom. Henry had looked up Benedict Arnold now, and got him separated from Arnold Bennett. Also he had found out all about the Bolsheviki and their revolution in Russia, and he told that history to the plain people of America, and that wasn't bunk either:

"All Jewish bankers are still in Russia. It was only the non-Jewish bankers who were shot and their property confiscated. Bolshevism has not abolished Capital, it has only stolen the Capital of the 'Gentiles'. And that is all that Jewish socialism or anarchism or Bolshevism is designed to do. Every banker who is caricatured with dollar marks on his clothes is a 'Gentile' banker. Every capitalist publicly denounced in Red parades is a 'Gentile' capitalist. Every big strike—railroad, steel, coal, is against 'Gentile' industry. That is the purpose of the Red movement. It is alien, Jewish, and anti-Christian."

## XLIV

Abner Shutt subscribed to the "Dearborn Independent", one dollar fifty per year, less than three cents per copy; it was the only magazine he had ever subscribed to, excepting the weekly paper of the Original Believers' Church. He read faithfully every word, and when the pamphlets were announced in the "Independent", he bought them— the first books he had purchased in his life, the family Bible having been a present to Milly when she was married. So much that was going on in the world had been mysterious to him, and now was explained! He talked about the subject, and got into arguments with shopmates who dared to dispute the truth.

Abner himself had never had much to do with Jews; but he now took to scanning the faces of the tradesmen who waited upon him, learning to recognize Jewish traits. He learned Jewish names from the "Dearborn Independent", and when he saw one over a store he did not enter. This meant that he had to do quite some hunting before he bought a new cap or a pair of socks in Highland Park.

He talked about the matter to the children, also, and warned them to have nothing to do with this evil race. It so happened that the boy who had led the gang of freight-car robbers had been named Levy, and of course that explained everything. It made Abner more inclined to mercy for his son, and Abner talked with him and got the names of men who were making money out of gambling, whiskey, and dope-selling in their home town. Some were Jewish names and some were not, but it was the Jews whom Abner fixed in his mind.

He also took notice of a school-teacher who dared to tell his boy Tommy that Mr. Ford's material about the Jews was not altogether reliable. The name of that young woman was O'Toole, but you couldn't tell from that, because Abner had been warned by Henry how often the Jews disguised their names. If you investigated you would probably find that this teacher had been born Otulinski, or some such outlandish thing.

In seeking this information Abner was not gratifying idle curiosity. A man had come to his home one evening, having got his name from the subscription list of the paper. This man represented a group of citizens who were not content with words, but meant to act. The traitors and revolutionists were organized; let Americans do the same. There had been a body called the Ku Klux Klan, which had served to put down Negro insurrection in the South—more history that wasn't bunk —and now it was being revived to put down Jews, Catholics, Reds, and other alien enemies. It was looking for men like Abner Shutt, and Abner said that he had been looking for this organization.

He paid twenty dollars, half a week's earnings, and was taken into a hall and draped in a white robe with a hood and a red cross on the front. He went through a solemn ceremonial and swore horrific oaths, meaning every word of them. He was taught secret passwords, and given the name and address of his "kleagle", and sent forth to gather information about traitors in America.

When he found one, a conference of the Klansmen would be held, and a sign would be prepared and nailed to the culprit's door, with crosses on it and a legend in red letters: "BE-WARE: THE KLAN RIDES". Now and then, for the benefit of all traitors collectively, hundreds of white-robed figures would gather in a field at night, bearing a huge cross made of combustible materials, and they would set it up and burn it for all the world to see. When those fires had died down, Abner went away assured that Protestant Gentile American civilization was safe.

## XLV

Henry went on digging up "dirt" about one Jew after another and spread it before the public gaze—never, of course, "without the strictest and fullest proof." Until at last he came to a Jew by the name of William Fox, producer of motion pictures. Henry assembled a grand lot of material concerning William's business methods and the moral character of his pictures; but, as it happened, the news of this inquiry leaked to William, and he sent a messenger to Henry to say that he too had been making an investigation. William had a newsreel service which went to many thousands of motion-picture theatres twice a week; and it had recently come to his notice that a great number of Ford cars were involved in accidents. He had instructed his hundreds of cameramen all over the country to get news of accidents involving Ford cars, and to get pictures of the wrecks with full details, how many people were killed, how many dependents were left, and so on. They were getting experts to swear what defect in each car had caused the accident. They would send in hundreds of pictures every week, and William would pick out the best ones to go into the newsreels.

The effect of this notice was immediate. Henry sent word back to William that he had decided to stop the attacks upon the Jews.

They were stopped; and Abner Shutt, the faithful subscriber, read no more about Jewish crimes. It didn't trouble him, because he had five bound volumes, which he could refer to from time to time. The Ku Klux Klan continued to burn crosses, and frightened out of that neighborhood several Jewish tradesmen who marked the prices of their goods too low, and several men who were suspected of visiting some woman they had no lawful right to.

A Jew named Sapiro had brought suit against Henry for five million dollars, charging libel. For years Henry used every legal device to keep the case from coming to trial; but finally all efforts failed; and, as part of the settlement, the motor magnate gave to the newspapers a statement to the effect that he had not hitherto had the time to read what was published in the "Dearborn Independent". Now he had been told by some of his friends that the "charges and insinuations" made against the Jews were untrue; he had been led for the first time to read the paper, and was "deeply mortified that this journal, which was intended to be constructive, had been made the medium for resurrecting exploded fictions." It was untrue that the Jews were in a conspiracy to dominate the world. The Protocols of the Learned Elders of Zion had been proved to be "gross forgeries", and if Henry Ford had known about their "general nature", he "would have forbidden their circulation without a moment's hesitation." Said Henry, beating his breast: "I deem it my duty as an honorable man to make amends for the wrong done to the Jews as fellow men and brothers, by asking their forgiveness for the harm I have unintentionally committed, by retracting so far as lies within my power the offensive charges laid at their door and by giving them the unqualified assurance that henceforth they may look to me for friendship and good will."

Very handsome indeed; but unfortunately for Henry's record, he had published an autobiography, a book entitled "My Life and Work," in which, speaking in the first person, he had espoused the entire anti-Jewish campaign, and summed up and endorsed the worst of the charges. In that book the Jewish influence stood described as "a nasty Orientalism which has insidiously affected every channel of expression." In that book Henry called upon the better Jews "to discard outworn ideas of racial superiority maintained by economic or intellectually subversive warfare upon Christian society." Writing about himself in his own autobiography, Henry declared that in his anti-Jewish articles he had exposed "false ideas, which are sapping the moral stamina of the people." He called upon the American people to "understand that it is not natural degeneracy, but calculated subversion that afflicts us."

Had Henry not known what he said in his own autobiography? Or had he now become so great that truth did not concern him?

## XLVI

Tom Shutt, the youngest, was now fifteen, and soon to enter high school. He was a sturdy lad—having had the good fortune to grow up in a time when the family had food. He had two large front teeth like his father, but he had his mother's blue eyes, and wavy brown hair which pleased the girls. He was beginning to think for himself, and was full of the cockiness inspired by that adventure. Abner found it annoying—because he wasn't thinking like Abner. He did not share the family sense of gratitude to Henry

Ford, but insisted that Henry had got more out of his workers than they had ever got out of him. He had no respect for the Klan, but on the contrary referred to it as a "racket". Abner proposed to "lam" him for this, but Milly had seen enough of that with Hank, and flung her arms around her boy and screeched.

Abner had to learn to hold his tongue and let his children say what they pleased. After he had talked it over with his friends, he decided that the blame lay with the teachers at the school; the "Reds" had got in among them, and were filling the minds of the children with "un-American ideas." Something was going to be done about that some day, the hundred percent Protestant Gentiles declared.

The Klan continued to "ride," and in fact was making up its mind to the longest ride of its career—all the way to the White House. All over the country the klansmen, who were also Ford customers, had taken up the idea of making Henry Ford their candidate. At home had been formed a "Dearborn Ford for President Club", which held meetings and filled the newspapers with propaganda. All the members wore hat-bands with a ribbon reading, "We Want Henry." One of these bands was presented to Abner free of charge, and it never occurred to him to ask whose money had paid for it. He had Milly sew it on his cap, and wore it proudly—even to work.

It was a strange kind of political campaign, for nobody knew whether the candidate was a Democrat or a Republican; the candidate wouldn't say, and probably didn't know. Henry went on making cars; a million and a half a year, climbing towards two mil-

lions. In spite of the fact that he lowered the price again and again, he was clearing an annual profit of a hundred million dollars; he had become a billionaire, one of two or three in the world.

Presently he turned out the ten millionth Ford, and started it on a pilgrimage of the United States; marvellous publicity, for wherever it came the people turned out to welcome it with parades and bands, and the proud owners of the most ancient Fords, those on which Abner had helped to screw the old carriage lanterns and to put in the stuffed cushions, brought them out from the back part of the barn, and went chugging out to welcome their great-grandchild. When this grandchild reached Hollywood, it made a tour of all the studios, and the movie stars came out to welcome it and have their pictures taken driving it.

Hundreds of Ford for President clubs were formed, and the straw ballots taken by newspapers and magazines showed Henry far in advance of all other candidates, even President Harding. Large sums were being spent in his behalf, but someone was very clever in concealing where the money had come from. Certainly Henry had nothing to lose, for there could be no better way to advertise a car than on the ballots in a national election. Wall Street was so afraid of his election that one man took out an insurance policy for four hundred thousand dollars against it.

President Harding, small-town politician surrounded by thieves, died of a broken heart, and the vice-president took his place. Here was the problem solved for both Henry and the Klan; here was their man already in office, a white Protestant Gentile hundred percent Vermont Yankee, close-fisted, close-mouthed, the strong, silent statesman, Cautious Cal. In the little mountain farmhouse where he was born they woke him up before dawn to take the oath of office, and hurried him off to Washington to take charge of a nation imperilled by grafters, speculators, Jews, Negroes, Catholics, and Bolsheviki.

Henry went to call on Calvin, and they had a highly secret conference. As a result of it, Calvin came out for Henry's project to buy Muscle Shoals from the government at a very low price; and in return Henry retired as a candidate for the presidency. "Keep cool with Coolidge," was the motto on which the Flivver King and the Klan proceeded to re-elect their choice.

## XLVII

Happy times were here again. American industry, adopting Henry Ford's policy of mass production and low prices, was making it possible for everybody to have his share of everything. The newspapers, the statesmen, the economists, all agreed that American ingenuity had solved the age-old problem of poverty. There could never be another depression. It was "the New Capitalism."

Henry had a seemingly inexhaustible market for his cars. He was employing more than two hundred thousand men, paying in wages a quarter of a billion dollars a year. He had developed fifty-three different industries, beginning alphabetically with aeroplanes and ending with wood-distillation. He bought a broken-down railroad and made it pay; he bought coal-mines and

trebled their production. He perfected new processes—the very smoke which had once poured from his chimneys was now made into automobile parts.

The Shutt family was a part of his vast empire, and they too were on the way up. Five days in the week, rain or shine, winter or summer, Abner's flivver came chugging to the Highland Park plant; he had a better one now, for the price was down to $300, and any workingman with a job could get one on monthly payments. Johnny had a brand new one of his own, which made the Shutts a "two-car family"—a great distinction, according to the motor-car ads.

Johnny, ever serious and hard-working, had finished at school and gone to work as a welder, a skilled job which paid him eight seventy-five a day. In less than a year he had become a sub-foreman, and was raised to nine fifty. That was what training did for you.

Strange and unexpected as it might seem, the second son was also "getting his". Hank did not have any title, and did not boast about his job, except to a few intimates. But he had the "dough", as he called it, also the "mazuma", and the "jack", and the "kale". He wore silk shirts and ties to match, razor-edged trousers, shiny new shoes, and an air of ease and confidence. He would come home and slip his mother a bill, and tell her to get something to make life easier for her; he would give his old grandpop a dollar or two to keep him in tobacco. He was a good-hearted fellow.

Hank would say he was working for the best people in Detroit; those whose names were in the blue-books and their pictures in the society columns. Right after the war the American people had plumped for prohibition; but these best people were taking the liberty of disregarding an inconvenient law. Right across a narrow river from Detroit lay a free country, well stocked with Canadian whiskeys and West Indian rums and French wines; the business of ferrying these products across the river at night was a lucrative one, and the job of moving them into the interior and hiding them before dawn, called for quick-witted young fellows who knew how to handle a truck, also an automatic or sawed-off shotgun in an emergency.

It was a far cry from the Original Believers' Church with its rigid doctrines of total abstinence, and the less Abner knew about his son's affairs the happier for him. Hank's work was done while Abner was sleeping the sleep of a worker on the "belt", a sound one. The only member of the family who knew about Hank's affairs was his sister Daisy, who stuck to him loyally, gave him wise advice, and tried to keep him out of the worst of his scrapes. It made a strange situation, for Daisy was a girl who went straight, and a faithful member of the church; yet she shared the secrets of the underworld of the Detroit area, and never betrayed them.

An ugly world, shocking to know about; as bad at the top as at the bottom, according to Hank. The police were crooked, the political game was a sell-out, if you had the cash you could buy anything or anybody. And Hank was out to "get his". He boasted that he was doing so, but it was a precarious kind of success, and his sister had more pity for him than trust. Was it the squint in his eyes which had given him a sense of inferiority, and caused him to expect opposition? Anyhow, Daisy loved this wayward brother, and listened to his stories and kept them locked in her heart.

Daisy had worked for a while in a "five and ten", and saved her money, and was now studying at a business college, learning the things that a secretary needs. She had needed no school to teach her the arts of a fine lady; all by herself she had found out the uses of silk stockings, of lipstick and rouge and a permanent wave. Nature had given her a fragile prettiness, and the impulse to use it while it lasted. Her eyes were fixed upon the higher regions, where in airy and elegant offices a stenographer makes the acquaintance of white collar workers and high-salaried executives. The Shutts, an American family, had no desire whatsoever to remain in the working-class, but meant to leave the hard and sweaty work of the world to those they called "hunkies" and "wops".

Tommy, the youngest, was in high school, and he too had discovered one of the trails leading to the heights. He was fleet of foot and quick of eye, and had done well as a quarter-back on the football team. It had been revealed to him that there were old graduates of the school who were interested in its success, and put up a little money for sweaters and travelling expenses, so that the sons of poor parents might pursue athletic careers.

Later on came a "scout" from the state university, where talent was even more appreciated. It was necessary to be discreet, for under no circumstances must football be professionalized; but if Tommy Shutt wished to come to Ann Arbor when he finished his high school course, friends would see to it that he had a job that would pay him a comfortable living, and not take more than three or four hours a week of his valuable time. Abner, coming home from eight hours a day pushing cotter-pins and spreading them, had listened to his son's crazy talk about going to college; when he learned about this offer, he realized that America was indeed the land of opportunity.

## XLVIII

Henry Ford was now getting close to his two million cars a year goal. Bringing coal from his West Virginia mines over his own railroad, bringing ore from his Michigamme mines in his own ships, he was showing the world an industrial miracle. From the moment the ore was taken out of the ship at the River Rouge plant, through all the processes of turning it into steel, and cutting the steel and shaping it into automobile parts with a hundred-ton press, and putting five thousand parts together into a car which rolled off the assembly line under its own power—all those processes were completed in less than a day and a half!

Some forty-five thousand different machines were now used in the making of Ford cars, in sixty establishments scattered over the United States. The various parts were carried in Henry's own ships to assembly plants in twenty-eight foreign countries. The Ford Model T would be put together in Yokohama or Buenos Aires, and its parts would be interchangeable; wherever you drove it, into the passes of the Himalayas or the jungles of the Chaco, you would find somebody who had learned to service and repair it. Henry was remaking the roads of America,

and in the end he would remake the roads of the world—and line them all with filling stations and hot-dog stands of the American pattern.

People would travel, and mingle, and learn to understand one another; they would see the best of everything, and want it, and in the end they would become sensible, and think sensible thoughts. Such had been Henry's plan, and at times he felt that he was succeeding. But more and more, as time passed, he was falling prey to doubts; losing his blithe optimism, and becoming glum and bitter. There were so many things in the world that were not to Henry's taste!

He had got himself a trusted writer-man, and had published several books full of sound advice and instruction for mankind. But it had not been enough; the thing which he called "nasty Orientalism" continued to spread. Girls went on wearing short skirts, people went on listening to jazz and dancing to it; they even began criticizing the Ford Model T, saying that it lacked beauty and grace, and that its colors were not sufficiently varied so long as they were black.

How could the country be saved from such evils? Henry consulted with his wife, a dignified lady who maintained an old-fashioned home, and engaged in charity according to Episcopal Church traditions. He consulted with Edison and others of his friends, and decided that what America needed was to be led back to its past; it must learn to appreciate what its forefathers had done. Henry was over sixty now, and as he looked back upon his boyhood, it seemed to him a time of peace and good fellowship, and his soul yearned towards it.

He started a vast museum of old-time America. He bought landmarks all over the country; the schoolhouse into which Mary's little lamb had followed her, and the village smithy about which Longfellow had written his poem. He restored whole villages in the old style, and moved scores of buildings to Dearborn and set them up, filled full of treasures; stage-coaches and covered-wagons and buggies, ancient locomotives and motor-cars, not forgetting the first Ford. He made some new purchase every week: a hundred-year-old bridge, a saw-mill, a fourteenth century cottage from England, some ancient funeral equipment, a three-legged stove, eighteen carriages, the hut of Charles P. Steinmetz. He established a market for Duncan Pfyfe chairs, spinning-wheels, jugs and drinking-cups, candlesticks, kerosene lamps, family albums, hoopskirts—in short, all the junk you had in your attic, provided it was old enough to be called "antiques". Drag it out, still with the dust on it, and write to Henry, and he would send an expert to look it over, and buy it and ship it to Dearborn.

Henry Ford was doing more than any man now alive to root out and destroy this old America; but he hadn't meant to do it, he had thought that men could have the machinery and comforts of a new world, while keeping the ideas of the old. He wanted to go back to his childhood, and he caused millions of other souls to have the same longing. Well-to-do ladies and gentlemen took to driving their costly limousines into remote mountain and wilderness roads, seeking ancient farmhouses which still had andirons and boiling-kettles and melodeons and "whatnots". They would purchase these treasures and carry them home, and set them up in modern houses by the side of jazz-painted private bars and self-refrigerating cocktail shakers.

Anyone would have thought that this was a mild and harmless occupation for a great man getting along in years; a safe hobby for him to play with in his second childhood. But troubles followed him even here. No way ever to escape troubles!

Some dangerously good salesman persuaded Henry to purchase a white cottage as "the birthplace of Stephen C. Foster," author of "Way Down Upon the Suwanee River," and other American folksongs. After the purchase had been made and a great ballyhoo set going, there appeared a niece and nephew of the composer declaring that the cottage in question was not the birthplace; and straightway the Flivver King found himself involved in a war. He was the most stubborn of men, and could not endure to admit that he had made a mistake; he even took the trouble to visit the aged daughter of the composer, then completely out of her mind. By "weeks of attention, flattery and suggestions" his agents persuaded her to make an affidavit which directly contradicted statements she had published when she was in her right mind.

The war spread among the Flivver King's own courtiers. They took to barring one another from the royal presence. They took to intriguing, forging interviews, even planting a fraudulent title examiner in the office of a country recorder of deeds. But the evidence piled up, and Henry, who had had his purchase announced over the radio as "not a reproduction, but the actual little white cottage in which Stephen C. Foster was born," had to change his catalogs and list item number 35 as just plain "Stephen Foster House." That was as far as he would go—although the fact was that neither Foster nor any member of the family had ever lived in that house, and it had been necessary to take off a large dormer window to make it look like the actual Foster house, long since torn down.

## XLIX

As a part of his crusade against the new America, Henry declared war upon that dreadful style of dancing which the international Jews and Bolsheviki had taught the American people for their undoing. Henry liked the clean and jolly "square dances" which the farm-people·had known when he was a boy. He found a dancing master in New England who had cultivated these almost forgotten arts, and brought him to Dearborn and put him on his payroll, and pretty soon there were classes learning the "Schottische" and the "Two-step", the "Lancers" and the "Quadrille", "Portland Fancy" and "Speed the Plow", and "Money Musk", which calls for six couples.

Also Henry searched out the old-time fiddlers, and got them together for tournaments. They played "Turkey in the Straw," and "Paddy on the Turnpike," and "Stony Country," and "Old Zip Coon," and "Two Dollars in my Pocket"; they taught these old tunes to children in the schools. In the Christmas season of 1925, in the main hall of the great new laboratory building at Dearborn, dedicated to research in the improving of motor-cars, the machines were moved back and covered with canvas. the floor was

waxed, and fifty couples, among them Henry and his wife, danced the "Virginia Reel". They had sent to Norway, Maine, for Grandpa "Mellie" Dunham, champion old-time fiddler, who sat, his toothless mouth hidden by white whiskers, sawing away at "Pop goes the Weasel" and "Lady Washington's Reel," "Fisher's Hornpipe" and "The Arkansas Traveller", while Henry's mechanics, executives and friends "shook a leg" to the delight of a great throng.

Henry talked freely to the newspaper reporters, and explained his ideas on this important subject. These old-time dances promoted friendliness, he said. "You cannot dance without coming in contact with at least seven human beings. You will clasp hands with them, you will get the human touch, the neighborliness that you have almost lost. America, the world, needs understanding of each other, the spirit of play." Henry declared that, just as he had got out a book about the running and repairing of his car, so now he was going to get out one about dances, complete and authoritative; old-fashioned dancing was going to be standardized, its parts made interchangeable, like Model T.

Abner and Milly and their friends at the church had danced when they were young, because they had liked to dance. Of late they had quit, because they were getting old and tired, and the young folks preferred the modern styles. But now Henry told them it was a patriotic action to dance the "Virginia Reel" and the "Lancers", and so they got together again. The Ladies' Auxiliary Society of the Original Believers' Church engaged a hall and an aged fiddler, and Abner and

Milly attended a dance for the first time since their marriage. As David danced before the Lord with all his might, so now Protestant Gentile America "sashayed" its partners before the ark of its old-time traditions.

But Abner and Milly went only once, for somehow the magic failed to work with them. Milly's health was weakening; and as for Abner, fate had played a scurvy trick upon him. At the very moment when his great master told him to dance, the master's underlings had fixed him so that he could hardly keep awake while driving his flivver home.

Things had been going so well with the Shutt family that the head of it had perhaps become a bit over-confident. He had a maggot always gnawing at his brain, the memory of those far-off days when he had been able to have personal dealings with Henry Ford. That summer evening away back in 1893, when he had escorted his father to the Bagley Street shed; the day in 1904 when he had tackled the big boss, alone and unaided, and got a job from him; the time in the following year when he had talked with him about spindle-nut screwing, and perhaps put the idea of an assembly-line into his head! The pleasant days of 1914, when the agent of the Social Department had come and advised his family, after having got his orders from Henry Ford direct. Could you blame Abner for thinking himself a bit more entitled to consideration than other men on the "belt"?

Twenty-two years now Abner had been working for Henry; and how many times he had been told, in Henry's own magazine, and also in "Saturday Evening Post" articles quoted in the newspapers, that merit and faithful service never went unrewarded in the Ford shops! Abner had been a sub-foreman years ago, and had proved that he could do the work. Was it not natural for him to dream that he might some day get back to his former status?

Moreover, in one of his newspaper interviews Henry had said that he didn't believe in gradations of rank and title in industry. Any one of his men could come to him at any time, or to the head of the man's department, or to any of the man's superiors. Abner had no chance to go to Henry now; there were many men working on the belt who had never seen the big boss, and would hardly have believed their eyes if he had come through the shop. But Abner knew the superintendent in charge of his particular assembly-line, and one day when the work was over he went to this man and in a few stammering sentences put his case.

Alas, Abner was breaking one of the strictest rules of the military discipline which governs these modern armies of production. He earned the furious resentment of his sub-foreman, who thought Abner had been trying to get his job—whereas Abner hadn't thought of that, it was some other sub-foreman's job he hoped for. The man began to "ride" him; he couldn't find much fault with the way Abner spread cotter-pins, but he could hold a stopwatch on him and raise hell if he stayed ten seconds more than his three minutes in the toilet, or if he stretched out his fifteen-minute lunch period while stuffing a last bite of sandwich into his mouth.

Flesh and blood couldn't stand it; one day Abner answered back, and was told to go and get his "time". There he was, after twenty-two years of merit and faithful service, deprived of all his honors and emoluments by a miserable straw-boss who had been with the company only a couple of years, and had never had so much as a nod from Henry Ford in his life. When Abner, in horrified protest, mentioned that he knew Mr. Ford, the man laughed in his face and told him to go straight to Henry's home on the River Rouge and complain!

## L

What Abner had to do was to go to his son, who managed to persuade somebody in the tool-shop to find his old man a place. The only vacancy was tending some grinding-machines; so Abner was on his feet again, feeding pieces of steel, all of uniform size and shape to the ten thousandth part of an inch, into machines which cut a groove in one side of them; Abner had to move from one machine to another, and when he finished at the last one, run back to the first, while the boss shouted: "Get a move on you, Shutt; we can't afford to have them grinders standing idle!"

Abner hadn't worked on his feet for years, and his legs had grown soft and his belly hung down in front. His calves began to hurt, and at night they were so swollen that he could hardly get to sleep. He didn't think he could stand it; but he had to stand it, because it was his living, his only chance. He was forty-eight years of age now, and had a boss who boasted in the magazines of kindness to his aged employees; if there was any other corporation head in America who made such

a claim, it hadn't come to Abner's attention, and if he got himself a reputation at Ford's for being a weakling and grumbler, how would he ever complete the payments on his new car?

It was those dreadful devices known as "the speed-up" and "the stretch-out." Every worker had to be strained to the uttermost limit, every one had to be giving the last ounce of energy he had in his carcass. Henry Ford would deny that, of course; he would write so blandly, so convincingly, about the purpose of scientific management being to ascertain exactly what each worker could do without strain, and to give him that much. It was a lie, it was a lie! Henry's workers wanted to scream when they read those articles of his. They were tired when they started in the morning, and when they quit they were grey and staggering with fatigue, they were empty shells out of which the last drop of juice had been squeezed.

It was that way everywhere, not merely at Ford's, but all through the cruel industry. Faster and faster, until the hearts of the men were seething with bitterness. All the motor-plants were in deadly incessant competition; every department in every plant competing with others, and with itself, with its own records in the past, with new "norms" which had been set by the engineers who watched the processes and designed new machines and techniques.

Did Henry Ford know about these conditions? Abner Shutt, faithful devotee, was sure that he couldn't know. Abner could read in the papers what the Flivver King was doing. He was traveling in Europe, inspecting his vast empire, and telling the people over there how to Americanize themselves. He was in Georgia, experimenting with fifteen thousand acres of golden-rod from which he expected to get rubber. He was on his huge farm in Michigan, growing soybeans, and watching his laboratory people making steering-wheels out of them. He was compiling his dance-book and collecting antiques for his museum. He was studying the thousands of birds for which he had provided air-conditioned homes. He was going everywhere and doing everything except watching the assembly-lines of his huge factory, with two hundred thousand slaves making themselves parts of machines—pick-up, push-in, turn, reverse—pick-up, push-in, turn, reverse, pickuppushinturnreverse, pickuppushinturnreverse—a man would go mad if he stopped to think about it.

Abner Shutt, patient and spavined old nag of industry, trotted back and forth in his treadmill, never daring to lift his eyes for one moment during eight hours, except for the exactly-measured fifteen minutes when the "ptomaine wagon" came along, selling fifteen-cent lunches for those who hadn't brought their own. Abner did his work, and held his tongue; he remembered the copy-book maxims about merit and faithfulness, and his lifetime devotion warred against the everyday facts about him, the bitter sneers he heard from the men—always under their breaths, of course, on account of the spies and stool-pigeons of the "service department".

But one thing Abner couldn't do, not even to oblige his kind boss, and that was to dance old-fashioned square dances after he got home from his work.

## LI

For eighteen years Henry had been making the Ford Model T. In the beginning he had had to fight for it against the world, and now of recent years the war had begun again. The sales force claimed that the old car was out of date; the public wanted new styles, new lines, new colors—and Henry's answer had been to go on making two million specimens every year, of any color that anybody wanted provided it was black. The roadster, when the top was raised, has as much style as an old poke-bonnet. The sedan was a square black box. The one-seater was named by the people a "coop", which may have been bad French, but was excellent American. All of these cars ran, and would be running twenty years from then, and that was what the American people wanted, said Henry Ford.

But Henry's rivals thought otherwise; they thought the American people wanted to keep up with their neighbors, and get ahead of them if possible. They thought the modern world wanted style, dash, swank, pep, zip, chic—the very number of such words indicated how many were thinking about the idea. They were demanding speed, and why not build cars with lines that suggested speed? As for color, the men were wearing fancy silk shirts and striped sweaters, and ties and socks to match; the women, not content with color in their clothes, were putting it on lips and toe-nails.

At the New York automobile show the dealers were now exploding into poetry in the effort to describe their wares. "The chrysalis of the butterfly is broken!" exclaimed one. "The hushed sweep of its floating swift travel," said the advertisers of Reo. The Jordan offered "a glorious yellow collapsible coupe." Buick boasted "a sporty roadster in grey upholstered in grey snakeskin leather." Dodge capped the climax with "a new roadster finished in rich cream color with deep blue hood and red striping."

This was what Henry meant by "nasty Orientalism"; and he did his best to keep it out of his moral shop. He was turning out his fifteen millionth black poke-bonnet, and sending it across the continent to be wined and dined. He continued to kick off his staff those executives who tried to persuade him to change his model. Year after year he had been kicking them out, whenever they dared oppose his will.

But there was a court of appeals which had more power even than Henry, and that was the car-buying public. Little by little the Chevrolets and the Plymouths crept up, while the Fords went down, and Henry had to reduce production, and turn off tens of thousands of men. The stubbornest great man in America kept on insisting that his car would never, never be changed; but by spring of the following year he saw that he was beaten, and that there would have to be a new Ford.

Good-bye to one more landmark of America! Those old "tin lizzies" were being driven on all the roads of the world, ten million of them at least; now gradually their numbers would decline, and the day would come when they would be as scarce as Civil War veterans. Henry figured that in the nineteen years of their history they had earned seven billions of dollars for those who had made them and served them; the value of the work they had done, who could compute?

## LII

A stupendous task confronted the Flivver King. Most of his forty-five thousand machines could turn out one thing and nothing else, and would have to be remodelled or else scrapped. Before any car part could be stamped, new dies would have to be cut; and there were more than five thousand parts. There would have to be a complete shut-down, except for the making of new parts for the old cars, which would continue at Highland Park. Henry would create a whole new industry at the River Rouge plant, with a million and a half feet of new floor space.

Among a hundred thousand men laid off, one humble spindle-nut screwer was too unimportant to be noticed. Abner went out and hunted odd jobs for a couple of months, and found a few, but not enough to keep from having to dip into his savings. Fortunately his son John was still employed, remodelling machines; and again he found a chance to speak a word for his old father. Abner was taken on as a sweeper, the lowest grade worker, hurrying here and there to carry off the scrap left by other men. But it was all right, he got the six-dollar minimum, and his family was safe again.

He watched some of the mighty labor going on, and heard about more of it. He saw huge machines picked up by electric cranes and deposited on flatcars to be taken to machine-shops for remodelling, or to River Rouge to be installed. Other parts went onto ships

—they were moving a whole tractor plant to Ireland. At River Rouge they built twenty-seven miles of conveyors to bring materials for the various parts, and to deliver the completed parts to the main assembly lines. They made new machines of power never before known. For the old plant, the stamping of frames had been done by a two hundred thousand pound press; for the new plant they built one two and a half times as big.

It was five months before this work was done; and meantime the automobile world had the great mystery of the age to speculate about. What was the new Ford going to be? What would it be named, how many horsepower would it have, how much would it cost? Henry knew, and his men at the top, but they kept their mouths shut. All Abner knew was what he read in the papers, which was something different every week. The new car had been completed, and was being tested —but hidden under the body of an old Model T, so that nobody could tell anything about it. Henry Ford himself was driving one, but only behind high fences. It was a high-powered car, and newspaper photographers tried to snap it with high-powered lenses.

The mystery was maintained until the very end. The new cars were in production; samples had been shipped to the show rooms, sewed up in canvas bags. Four hundred thousand advance orders were booked, a pig in a poke. On the day the car was released for sale, the Ford Motor Company began a five-day series of advertisements in five thousand newspapers throughout the country. Henry told that the New Model A had a standard gearshift and fourwheel brakes; also that it had "low

smart lines", and "a bit of the European touch in its coachwork and its contour." Alas for old-time America!

In New York the car was shown to a fashionable audience in the Waldorf, by salesmen in evening dress. Next day a quarter of a million people stormed the doors of seventy-six dealers; traffic was blocked in the streets, and it was necessary to hire Madison Square Garden for a week, so that the public could satisfy its curiosity. The public learned that it could have any color it wanted provided it was dark Arabian sand with light Arabian stripe, or Gun Metal blue with French grey stripe, or Niagara blue with French grey stripe, or Dawn grey, still with French grey stripe. "Nasty Orientalism" had won out; it was so successful that Henry had to make a million cars in the first six months.

## LIII

Abner Shutt was back at spindlenut screwing, the work which he knew. He screwed on a fashionable car now, and felt that his social status had been raised. But he paid for it, because his work was at River Rouge, and he had to drive a score of miles every day; not so economical, nor so pleasant in winter.

The children went on climbing the social ladder. John Crock Shutt had been promoted to the class which receives a monthly salary instead of a weekly wage. He had met the daughter of his department head and got engaged to her; the young couple were making arrangements to buy a home in a neighborhood so elegant that his parents would be embarrassed to drive their old flivver into it.

Daisy, too, was on the way to achieving her heart's desires. She had obtained a position in the office of a concern which made cushions for Ford cars. She was getting twenty-three fifty a week, and she learned her job, and made her employer's interests her own according to the best copy-book maxims. She came home every evening full of gossip as to what was going on in this little satellite industry; before long her parents knew the names, the appearance, the earnings of a whole staff of executives and clerks who supervised and recorded the making of cushions.

A different sort of report concerning Hank. His business, too, was thriving, but Abner and Milly had not been told much about it. Now, however, came an event which broke into the newspapers; the boy had got into a shooting affray, and was lodged in jail, charged with manslaughter. Daisy explained to her parents that it wasn't Hank's fault; he wasn't a criminal, but a hero, who had been defending his employer's property against a bunch of hijackers. The fact that the "property" was a truckload of liquor was hardly gratifying to devout members of the Reverend Orgut's church.

This was a problem beyond the power of Abner and his pastor. But Hank had powerful friends by now; a shrewd lawyer was obtained, and when the trial came off, there were witnesses who testified that they had been playing pool with Hank at the time of the shooting, and he was acquitted. He disappeared from town for a while—until, in due course, the leader of the hijackers had been shot. Then he turned up again, jaunty as ever, and old Tom had his pocket money again,

and Daisy knew all the inside affairs of the bootlegging ring which ruled Detroit.

Tommy was continuing his career as football player at the high school; finishing the season in a blaze of glory by kicking a goal from the field. Such sudden fame was a strain upon a young fellow's character, but Tommy seemed able to stand it, and John and Daisy, who were achieving success in the real world, helped to keep him from getting a swelled head. He had grown up to be a good-looking fellow with wavy brown hair, a reddish complexion, and a strong tendency to freckles. He was what his parents called a "good" boy, and withstood the temptations of athletic life; but he had not outgrown the tendency to criticize which had been implanted by his "Red" teachers. He would make remarks about the feudal lord of Dearborn which seemed in the nature of blasphemy to his worshipful family.

But there were many who felt as Tommy did, and not only in the schools. The "Reds" published papers, and there were trouble-makers and sneerers in the plant, more and more of them. The "Kluxers" had become inactive, and it was clear, even to Abner's slow mind, that they had not succeeded in forcing all Americans to be patriotic. There was something wrong with the country; but since Henry had discontinued publishing the "Dearborn Independent", Abner no longer had a chance to find out what it was.

## LIV

The reign of Cautious Cal came to its dignified end, and there was a new President, known as the "Great Engineer." All the masters of industry supported him, Henry Ford among them, and Abner read in his newspaper what they said about him, and agreed that he was exactly the sort of man a great business country like America needed at the head of its affairs. The "New Capitalism" was blooming like a sunflower, and money was almost free. The Flivver King gave one of his rough and ready newspaper interviews, in which he said that nowadays a young man wouldn't get rich by saving his money, but by spending it. "Two cars in every garage and two chickens in every pot," agreed Herbert Hoover.

The Shutt family was the sort that Henry and Herbert approved. It was now a "three-car family," since Hank had got a fast one, and went about with a gun in his pocket settling various difficulties for his boss. It was near to becoming a "four-car family", for Tommy was at the point of deciding that it didn't look quite right for a quarterback on the team to arrive at school on a bicycle.

But in the first year of the Great Engineer's reign there appeared a cloud in the sky. Only a little one, to be sure, and Abner Shutt didn't know enough to worry about it; rather he welcomed it, having been taught by his employer to distrust Wall Street and the "international bankers", most of them Jews. When Abner read in the evening paper about a terrible panic on the stock exchange, and how billions of "values" had crumbled to nothing in a few hours, he said: "Serves 'em right. Them fellers ain't never earned the money."

That might be true, but it did not alter the fact that them fellers were the ones who had been spending the money, and now they would have to stop. Them fellers were not merely Wall Street speculators, they were small town merchants, even bootblacks and soda jerkers, and farmers who had telephones and had been calling up some branch house of a brokerage firm and playing the market for a rise. All over America that had been going on, it was the automatic result of theories of easy and perpetual prosperity preached in the newspapers. If the profits were there, and if they were so certain, why shouldn't the plain people have a share? Why leave it all to Wall Street?

So the plain people had reasoned, and now they had got themselves "wiped out". They couldn't buy the new Ford they had been planning for; if they had already bought it, they couldn't meet the payments. This sickening discovery, made by millions of people all the way from Bangor to San Diego, constituted a new economic fact which took a long time to work itself out, and to be realized by big business men and their newspaper editors and economists.

The first panic lasted several days; then it passed, and there was a lull, full of anxiety. President Hoover called a council of business leaders to discuss what was to be done, and these big medicine men assembled, and agreed that the country must have confidence, and they told the country to have it. Henry Ford attended, and when it was over he showed them the way; handing to the newspaper men a statement that the Ford Motor Company had so much confidence in the future of America that it was raising the minimum wage in its plants to seven dollars a day.

A grand gesture, which brought Henry more of those rousing cheers which he had learned to use in his business of selling cars. There were only a few soreheads to point out that since Henry had established his five-dollar minimum, sixteen years back, the cost of living in the Detroit area had nearly doubled, so that the new seven-dollar wage was far less than the old one had been. Nor had Henry said how many men were going to get the new wage; there was nothing to keep him from turning off men, and this he proceeded to do immediately. Before the announcement he had been paying the six-dollar minimum to two hundred thousand men; right after it he was paying the seven-dollar minimum to a hundred and forty-five thousand. Multiply and subtract, and see how much Henry was helping to increase the purchasing power of the American workers!

## LV

John Crock Shutt had become a specialist in "resistance welding" in the enormous tool-shop of the River Rouge plant. This was a new and quite marvellous process which made various automobile parts into solid pieces of steel. John was all wrapped up in the details of it, and during working hours thought of nothing else; during his other hours he liked to talk about it, or to read technical papers about steel. They were making new kinds every day, and the more you knew, the higher your salary would rise.

John was round-faced, rosy, contented and shining with prosperity. He was married to a fashionable young lady who had been through high school, belonging to a secret society which had secured her from contact with undesirable classmates. The young couple had bought a home in a tract having restrictions which protected them from meeting persons who could not pay eight thousand dollars for a residence. John and Annabelle were making payments of seventy-five a month, plus interest; the "villa" was showy, but jerry-built for all that, and its owners would have heavy repair bills in the future. But they didn't worry; being sure that so long as men rode in automobiles, John's special knowledge would command its price.

These two young people had been raised under a system of industrial feudalism. If anybody had said that to them, they would have taken it as an affront; but the fact was that their minds were shaped to a set of ideas, as rigidly and inevitably as the steel parts which the plants were turning out by the million. It was a hierarchy of rank based upon income. Annabelle associated with wives of her own level, carefully avoided those of lower levels, and crudely and persistently sought access to those of higher levels. Below her were the serfs of industry, the hordes of wage-earners; above her were higher executives, and at the top the owners, the ineffable, godlike ones about whom everybody talked incessantly, gleaning scraps of gossip and cherishing them as jewels.

The Ford empire was not a metaphor but a fact, not a sneer but a sociological analysis. Henry was more than any feudal lord had been, because he had not merely the power of the purse, but those of the press and the radio; he could make himself omnipresent to his vassals, he was master not merely of their bread and butter but of their thoughts and ideals. John had been trained to make steel for Henry, and also to admire and reverence him. The more John did these things, the more he prospered, and the more he prospered, the more he admired and reverenced. From the point of view of John and Annabelle it was a most virtuous circle.

The same was true of all the other members of the Shutt family, striving to make their way in a world which existed for and by the motor-lords and money-lords of the Detroit area. Abner and Milly were the most abject of serfs, having pictures of their liege cut from Sunday supplements and pasted on the wall, serving the same purpose as Russian ikons. They were blissful in the knowledge that their oldest son was attaining rank in Henry's service, and that Daisy was in love with a promising young bookkeeper in Henry's administration building. It was their hope that Tommy's youthful rebelliousness would pass and that he too would become one of Henry's retainers; realizing that whatever might be wrong was due to vicious underlings who abused the trust of the great and good Lord, who was stern but just, and merciful with wisdom.

Furthermore, it was true that whether you served the master or rebelled against him, he still dominated your life. That was true of Henry Ford Shutt, a sort of outlaw, a Robin Hood hiding in Sherwood Forest. Hank, with his twisted mind, jeered at all the great ones, and insisted that they were crooks and grafters like himself. But even so, did he not take dangerous journeys by night so that they might have liquor for their cocktail parties? Had he not risked his life more than once to defend their property? Henry Ford did not drink nor serve liquor in his home; but most of his executives did, and Henry himself had need of other services, which Hank was finding out about. It would not be long before he too would delight his old father's heart by coming under the banner of the Flivver King.

## LVI

There came another panic; there came several more, at intervals long or short. American business began to slow up, and then to sicken and die. Sales began to fall off, dealers to cancel their orders; fear spread from retailers to wholesalers, then to shippers and manufacturers, then to the primary sources of raw materials and power. Profits vanished, and the values of stocks declined. "The market has no bottom any more," said the brokers, and turned off their employees, shut up their offices, and went down to the East River docks and jumped in, or mounted in the elevators to the roofs of their office-buildings and threw themselves over the parapets.

From the time of the first crash to its climax was a period of three years and a half, practically all the reign of the Great Engineer. It ruined poor Herbert's life, for he knew it wasn't his fault, yet he had to carry the blame. The only thing he could think of was to have Congress vote huge sums to his friends and beneficiaries, the great banks and corporations which had put up his campaign funds. The theory was that this money would seep down to the consumers and promote trade. But what happened was that the money stayed right in the banks where he put it; they couldn't lend it unless they could see a chance of profit, and how could a business man promise a profit when he couldn't find anybody who had money to spend? It was the end of an era.

The first and most obvious economy for any American who found his bank account running low was to go on driving his old car instead of turning it in for a new one. So the first industry to be hit was that of making cars. In a little more than a year there were estimated to be 175,000 men out of work in Detroit alone. The city was caring for forty thousand destitute families, and had accumulated a deficit of $46,000,000.

Naturally, the motor-car manufacturers had to reduce the surpluses they kept in the banks, and the plain people had to draw out money to keep alive from week to week. So one day Abner Shutt, coming out from work, bought his evening paper from the customary newsboy, and saw a headline about a bank in trouble, and it was the institution in which he kept his savings. Trembling with fear he ran to his dingy flivver, one of the many thousands of Model Ts lined up in the area provided. He drove in haste to the bank, but of course it was after closing hours, and all he could do was to stand and ask questions of other persons as much frightened as he was, and as ignorant.

A bank crash! Abner had thought of this great institution with its imposing marble columns and bronze railings in the same way that he had thought of Henry Ford, and the United States government, and his God who was going to take care of his eternal future; all four were permanently established things, above and beyond the ken of poor working people. Now he learned that a bank could fail, and that the government took charge of it, and nobody could get any money, at least for a time. But it would be all right in the end, said the newspapers, soothingly; mention of such subjects always closed with the statement that America was sound, and that everything was coming out all right in the end, and all that was needed was "confidence."

Next morning, early, Abner explained his plight to the foreman, and asked for a couple of hours to go and try to get his money out of the bank. The man's answer was cordial: "All right, Shutt, you go and tend to your banking business, but you better get your time before you go, because we need men that can stay on the job, and I been seeing for a long time that you can't keep up the pace."

There was Abner, standing in the middle of the floor with tears streaming down his cheeks, pleading with that boss, telling again the long story of how he had worked for the great and good Lord Henry—it was now twenty-eight years, and surely that oughter give a man some bit of a claim. "My God, mister, I got a wife an' family, and what 'm I gonna do?"

But the foreman had become adamant. The situation was that he had received orders to turn off a dozen men that day, and had been figuring in his mind how to select them, and here this poor devil had gone and selected himself; stuck his head out, and whack, down came the axe. A boss is only human, after all, and doesn't like to see an old bugger tottering along, trying to tend a row of machines half the length of a city block, and falling behind and having to be bawled out all the time. If a shop has to economize, a good place to begin is in a foreman's lungs!

Nearly a score of years back, in Henry's days of idealism, he had had a census taken in his plant, and finding that the percentage of older men in his employ was less than that of the population, he had ordered his managers to find jobs for more old men. But now the world had changed. Henry's plant was ten times as big, and Henry himself was old; he left his troubles to others, and avoided knowing what they were doing.

## LVII

So there was Abner on the street again, in such a mood that he would not have cared if one of the cars speeding on the boulevard had crashed into him and sent him to kingdom come. He went to the closed bank and stood round for a while, exchanging mournful words with others in the same plight—it wasn't long before all the banks in Detroit were closed, and fifty thousand families were in the boat with the Shutts. There was a sign on the door saying that the bank was closed by order of the Federal examiner. If you wanted to know more, spend money for a newspaper—if you had that much out of the bank.

Abner couldn't bear to take this bad news home. He drove to other motor-plants and factories. Men who had been fired from Ford's at seven dollars a day could often go to one of the concerns which made parts for Ford and get work at two or three dollars a day. That was another of the tricks which

Henry was playing upon his workers, and upon the public which read his newspaper interviews. More and more he was farming out the making of parts, and always on such terms that the place which made them became a sweatshop. Nobody could hold Henry responsible for wages paid to those who made his cushions, or tires, or speedometers, or windshield-wipers, or other gadgets.

But none of these concerns was "hiring" just now; most of them had guards who wouldn't even let you get to the office to inquire. "Nothin' doin', bo." Sometimes there were long lines, and Abner could see how many better men than himself were on the market. He was now fifty-three, and had grey hair, and heavy lines of care in his face, and a shuffling gait—in short, Abner Shutt was licked before he started.

He would join the class of men who went about tending furnaces in winter and lawns in summer, and picking up other odd jobs. People expected you to do that sort of work for a dollar a day or less; there were men ringing your door-bell all the time who were ready to do any sort of work for the price of a meal. The well-to-do would point that out to the men they were hiring; after which they would go off to a bridge party or a dinner, where the problems of the time were discussed, and they would say that most of these unemployed wouldn't work if you gave them a chance.

Other members of the Shutt family still had their pay each week. But Daisy had just got married to her bookkeeper; and what a wedding present the cushion company handed her! Daisy's superior told her that he was sorry, but they were under orders to drop two hundred employees, and all married women were on the list.

So now Daisy had to live on the wages of a bookkeeper who was working two days a week, and had no certainty of even this much. The most obvious economy for the young couple was to board with her parents, who had a house fully paid for. Daisy got into the little "coop" which she and her husband had bought, and drove all day looking for work. When she had made good and certain that there was no work for a young married woman, she set out to sell the "coop", and found that so many persons had had the same idea that the market was glutted; thousands of used cars were being shipped out of the Detroit area to keep the price from dropping to zero. In the end she took forty-two dollars for a car which had been purchased for two hundred and twenty-five.

## LVIII

A hundred thousand families in that neighborhood were occupied as the Shutt family were—trying to figure out some way to raise a little cash. The poorest were begging for a nickel to pay for a sandwich; the richest were trying to borrow a million to save a bank or an industry. There had come to be a fashion in the highest social circles; whereas in the old days the speculator or the financier had boasted of how much he had cleaned up in a certain deal, he now boasted of how much he had lost. A strange kind of distinction, but the only kind there was.

When goods are scarce the price goes up; and when money is scarce the price of everything else goes down. Abner and Milly spent days and nights of misery, conferring together in the effort to cheat that economic law. Since neither of them knew anything about such laws, it was impossible for them to realize what had happened to the value of houses, furniture, cars. When Abner and Daisy went out to try to sell or pawn something, Milly would scold because they had not got a better price. She had been so penurious, hanging on to every penny, complaining all the time about the young people who wanted to spend it. Now whether you had saved it or spent it seemed all the same.

They couldn't afford even the taxes on their house, and wanted to sell and move into lodgings. But what could you get for a house in Highland Park? Henry Ford had played a trick on that town when he had moved his big plant to River Rouge, ten or twelve miles away; all his workers had tried to sell their homes at the same time, and values had dropped to nothing. Now two-thirds of the people of the town were out of work, and you couldn't find anybody to lend even a few hundred dollars on real estate.

They decided that the solution of the problem lay in renting rooms. They crowded up, and began the unhappy business of trying to get money out of workingmen who themselves were terrorized by a scarcity of jobs. Men would think up any scheme to get a roof over their heads and some food in their stomachs, even for a few days; and poor Milly wasn't very good at seeing through such schemes. Presently they got a likely young fellow who had a job; but it wasn't long before he was making advances to Daisy, a respectable young married woman

who went to church. When she re-
pelled him he got sore, and paid her
back by doing the family out of about
fifteen dollars.

Poor old Tom, who had become
helpless with his rheumatism, died in
the first winter of this depression.
They were able, with the help of the
children, to give him a burial; but
when the old grandmother followed
him a year later they had to bear the
disgrace of letting the county bury her.
Such things do not seem much to outsiders, but they are what break the
spirit of poor people who have always
earned what they spent and kept themselves "respectable". Abner had come
now to the point where he had to forget that his second son was a bootlegger and a gangster, and let Milly
take gratefully whatever money Hank
brought. Unfortunately Hank's business also had been "shot"; the customers were all buying the cheaper
grades, he said.

Even the football industry was in
trouble. The open-handed "old boys"
of the alumni began making excuses
like everybody else, and the athletic
committee passed these excuses on to
the players. Tommy had made good
as a quarterback, nobody had any fault
to find with him, said the committee,
but there just were not any more easy
jobs, and he would have to tend furnaces and wait on tables. Half a year
of that was enough to change his attitude to college life; with his father and
mother not knowing where to get
money for food, Tommy decided he
hadn't so much time for football. Since
he had to do real work, he would do
real studying too, and see what there
was to be got out of a college education.

## LIX

That prosperous and self-satisfied
young couple, the John Crock Shutts,
had been living for three years in their
two-story home of yellow brick, with
tiled bathrooms and an oil-furnace and
a nursery for their two babies. Seventy-five dollars a month plus interest
they had obligated themselves to pay,
and it was one of those "Michigan
land contracts," in which the seller
keeps the deed until the full amount
has been paid. And now, right while
Annabelle was in the midst of prepa-
rations for a bridge party, her husband
received notice that his trained services
could no longer be used by the Ford
Motor Company.

They were in a most dreadful panic.
They had almost no cash. They could
not look to Annabelle's father, who
had got badly caught in the market.
They could borrow a little on John's
life insurance policy, but not nearly
enough. They had something like a
hundred and sixty dollars a month in
instalments and interest to pay on
house, furniture, and new Model A
Ford.

John moved heaven and earth trying
to get some kind of a job. He no
longer asked anything for his skill; he
was willing to take whatever he could
get; and on those terms he obtained a
job in the same department of the
River Rouge plant from which he had
been let out. He did much the same
kind of work; only instead of getting
three hundred and a quarter a month,
he got the six-dollar minimum—Henry
had reduced it by now—and the plant
worked only Mondays, Tuesdays and
Wednesdays. Eighteen dollars a week!
There was no chance of the little

family's meeting all those payments. They had to give up the house, on which they had paid about thirty-eight hundred dollars; they had to give up the furniture, and the new electric refrigerator, and the car, which had been for Annabelle—John still had an older one, which he needed to get to his work. They had to move their few belongings into one-half of a two-family house in a disgusting workingclass neighborhood, to which Annabelle couldn't invite any of her friends. Instead of giving bridge parties, she had to scrub the floors and wipe the noses of her two babies. John was right back where he had been born—one generation from shirtsleeves to shirtsleeves!

There is a cruel saying that when poverty comes in at the door, love flies out at the window; and it looked as if it might apply to this case. Annabelle, who had been fighting so aggressively to advance her husband's social position, now turned her balked energies to finding fault with him. She didn't know enough to blame the social system, she blamed those about her, and her attention became centered upon the fact that her husband had been giving money to his family. She made it her business to see that those relatives didn't get another penny. Let that handsome football-playing brother go to work! Let them get something out of their bootlegger and gangster!

Annabelle knew all about Hank, because he had been arrested again and had got his picture in the paper. It was something about an election charge —he had been intimidating voters, it was said. Oddly enough, he had been working for a candidate who had the support of Henry Ford, and was said

to have the company's financial backing. What could that mean?

Annabelle didn't know, or care, for she had turned against the great Lord of Dearborn also. He might fool the Shutt family, but he couldn't fool her. The peremptory firing of John had been just a dirty trick to reduce his pay without admitting it. It was a scheme they were working everywhere throughout the plant; Annabelle heard of it again and again, and presently her own father admitted it to her, and said he had orders to carry it out. Oh, yes; great capitalists like Henry Ford didn't care a thing about money, they worked just for the pleasure of providing people with good cars! "He makes me want to puke!" said Annabelle, whose language was not so refined when she was angry.

## LX

The Flivver King had his side of the case. He had been the one in America who could boast of the greatest gains, and now he was the one who could boast of the greatest losses. In the years 1924, '25 and '26, he had made more than a hundred million net profit per year. The reorganization of his plant had set him back sixty millions in 1927, and as much in the following year. But in 1929 the new Model A had turned this into sixty millions profit. In 1930 he had managed, by prompt firing of men and speeding up of the others, to stave off the effects of the depression and make another sixty millions. But by 1931 nothing could avail against the mounting tide of disaster; the Ford Motor Company lost fifty-three million dollars, and in the following year it lost seventy-five millions.

The story was told in the record of Henry's car sales. In the last three years of the old Model T he had sold close to two million a year. He had sold nearly two million of Model A in 1929. But in the next year his sales dropped off to a million and a half. In 1931 he stopped giving out production figures, but it was known that his sales of passenger cars were down almost to half a million.

To be sure, Henry could stand it as no other manufacturer in the United States, for he had three hundred millions of cash reserves. But how long was this depression going to last? Henry backed up Herbert loyally in his "confidence" preachments, but in his secret heart he knew that neither of them had any idea what lay ahead. Hold on to your money!

What turned Detroit so bitterly against Henry Ford was not that he worked his men hard and turned them off fast, but the hypocrisy with which he operated. Go ahead and be a business man, and save your own skin if you can, but for God's sake stop trying to make us think you are a philanthropist! Stop this holy talk in the newspapers! Stop the untrue statements about what you are doing and what you mean to do!

Henry wanted the public to believe that good times were on the way back, because that would give people confidence and cause them to buy cars. All right, that was a business device that every manufacturer in the land understood, and was using every time he made a speech. But was it sporting of Henry to give out the announcement that on account of the excellence of his new models and the certainty of increasing sales, he was taking on ten or twenty thousand new men? To have that featured in the papers, and have a mob of poor devils from the breadlines and the flophouses come piling over to River Rouge—other poor devils riding in open freight trains in the bitterest winter weather—and when they got to the gates of the plant, find a swarm of "service men" with clubs in their hands and guns on their hips, stopping all the men who didn't have badges, driving them away with a stick in their backs, or, if there were too many of them, turning streams of icy water on them from high-powered hoses? Certainly it was an odd consequence of extreme popularity, that you had to have the toughest gangsters to drive people away from you!

## LXI

It had been eighteen years ago that Henry Ford had stepped out into the limelight as a model employer, a guide and instructor to all other American employers. In that time he had published four books bearing his name, several scores of magazine articles, and no one could say how many interviews. Now it was time to ask how his theories had worked out. The answer was that Henry Ford was the most hated man in the motor-car industry. One of his workers would pay a nickel for the "Saturday Evening Post", and come on an article about the ideal conditions in his plant, and the man would throw the magazine on the floor and wipe his greasy boots on it.

For years Henry had been telling the world that the use of machinery did not cause unemployment; and now look! At the River Rouge plant they were putting in new machines as fast as they could design and make them. Twenty men who had been making a certain part would see a new machine brought in and set up, and one of them would be taught to operate it and do the work of the twenty. The other nineteen wouldn't be fired right away —there appeared to be a rule against that. The foreman would put them at other work, and presently he would start to "ride" them, and the men would know exactly what that meant.

What pretexts they used to get rid of men! Next door to Abner Shutt lived an old fellow who had worked for the company seventeen years, and had been told to turn in his badge because he started to wipe the grease off his arms a few seconds before quitting time. Down the street lived a young fellow who had been an errand-boy and had made the mistake of stopping to buy a chocolate-bar. They had a thousand petty regulations on which the "spotters" could take you up. A foreman had talked with one of his men; that was against the regulations, and out he went. Two men had talked to one another while at work; out they both went. You were fired for forgetting to wear your badge on your left breast, for staying too long in the toilet, for eating your lunch on the floor, for talking to men in the new shift coming on. It wasn't even necessary that you had done one of these things; it sufficed that some ex-pugilist of the "service department" said that you had. There was no appeal.

If you were smart and remembered all the regulations, they fired you another way; you were not needed right now, they said, but keep your badge, you were still on the payroll, and

they'd let you know when they were ready. That way they kept up their statistics; but it meant that you couldn't get a job anywhere else, because the new boss would ask where you had worked last, and would call up Ford's to inquire, and of course he didn't want some fellow who was on the Ford payroll.

With every month of the depression these things had got worse and worse. The twenty-five thousand workers were driven until they went out "punch-drunk". Sometimes one went out on a stretcher, because men so driven couldn't handle machinery without accidents. On no subject had Henry written more eloquently than the importance of safety; but again and again his "safety department" was overruled by his speed-up department, and there was a saying in the plant that it took one life a day. They had their own hospital, and there was no way to get any figures.

## LXII

Henry Ford was now nearly seventy; he was the richest man in the world, and the perfect embodiment of a point of view known as "economic determinism." He had started out with such a fine set of ideals, so much benevolence in his heart, so many resolves to make his life count for good; and here he was a billionaire—and his money held him like a fly caught in a spider's web. The most powerful man in the world was helpless in the grip of a billion dollars. It had made him into something he had never dreamed of being. It was master, not merely of his actions, but of his thoughts, so that he didn't know what he had become; he was blind, not merely to the realities of his business, but to those of his own heart.

He had preached industry, made it his religion; work, work was man's salvation, production was God. Now the Flivver King had the most wonderful machine of production in the whole world—and it stood idle nine-tenths of the time. He had trained two hundred thousand men to look to him for the means of working—and now he had to hire many thousand others to drive them away from him with clubs and guns. He had made a million people dependent upon him for their daily bread, and he left them to rot in garrets and cellars and empty warehouses, in shacks made of tin and tar-paper, in holes dug in the ground—any place so long as they did not get in the way of Henry!

He had once been simple and democratic; but his billion dollars now decreed that he should live like an Oriental despot, shut off by himself, surrounded by watchmen and guards. He who had liked to chat with his men and show them the work now would not dare to walk past his own assembly-line without the protection of secret service men. He who had been so talkative had now grown morose and moody. His only associates were "yes-men", those who agreed with everything he said. He met few strangers, because everybody was trying to get some of his money, and he was sick of being asked. His secretaries helped to keep him alone, because he had made a fool of himself so many times, they could never be sure what he would say next.

He stayed in his big stone house and his private park, with the trees and flowers and birds which he loved. These could be counted upon to behave themselves if you treated them right—unlike the malicious and ungrateful world of men. Children, old-fashioned dances, and fiddlers playing jig tunes, these things soothed the heart of the unhappy old Flivver King. But the children who came to his parties must be well-fed and happy; let nobody mention the ten thousand starvelings who came every day to the children's bread-lines in the city of Detroit! Let nobody bring up that sorest of all subjects, the claim of the city administration that Henry ought to share some of the burden of feeding these children, since so many of their parents were unemployed Ford workers. Since all Henry's plants lay outside Detroit, he did not have to pay it any taxes, and the city thought that wasn't fair.

There had been a perfectly good administration of the city, one which Henry had financed, and which had done his will. But the people had not been satisfied, they had recalled Henry's mayor, and elected one of their own choice, an Irish Catholic judge by the name of Murphy who was what Henry called a demagog, a sentimentalist, a stump-speaker, all those things which spelled the odious word "politics". Now Detroit had what it wanted, and Henry left it to stew in its own juice.

The "demagog" mayor appointed an "unemployment committee", which made a statement that the city was paying seven hundred and twenty thousand dollars a year to keep Henry Ford's unemployed alive. The city welfare department charged that he had turned off the fathers of five thousand families, with never a move for their aid.

The great industrialist and improver of mankind lost his pleasure in a dancing-party, and his son Edsel, who didn't ordinarily bother about newspaper stories, gave a long statement to the New York "Times", attempting to disprove the charge. What was a Ford employee anyhow? For how far back was the company responsible for those who had once worked for it? The implication would seem to be that the company did assume responsibility for those who had been recently employed. Abner Shutt, for one, would have been very glad to get such a message from his employer's son; but for some reason that was not included in the statement.

### LXIII

Some time after the war the government had sought to get rid of a fleet of cargo-boats which had been built to supply the army, and for which world commerce had no use. Henry had bought a hundred and ninety-nine of them, and brought them to River Rouge and scientifically wrecked them, finding a place for everything in his huge plant. He hadn't expected to make money, but it had amused him, the way it amuses other men to solve cross-word puzzles. Henry's passion was for saving things, and finding out how to do things.

With those boats had come the men who had been in charge of them; and as each boat was wrecked, there was another group of men to be placed in the Ford empire—another kind of problem which interested Henry. Among them was a well-known boxer in the navy, Harry Bennett by name; he was hard of face and of fist, and

had a quality which had been the basis of law and order under the ancient system of feudalism—when he hired himself to a man, he made his master's cause his own. Henry, living under the modern feudalism of industry, felt the same need which had caused the Sultan of Turkey to establish his Janissaries, and the princes of renaissance Italy their Condottieri; to protect him and his billion dollars required an army of well-equipped and trained fighting men.

Bennett became the head of Henry's "service department"—a title which could have been given only after the billion dollars had extracted all the humor from its owner's heart. It was Bennett's job to organize and train the thirty-six hundred private police who guarded the gates of the plant, watched the work in every department, reported violations of many hundreds of regulations, and, as spies, mingled with the men, detecting grumblers and kickers, union organizers and "Red" agitators. Such work had to be done not merely inside the plant but elsewhere. If a labor leader came to town, Henry's service department must know where he went and with whom he talked. In other words, Henry Ford's army set up an intelligence bureau, with spies and counterspies, essential in every war. Since the best defensive is always an offensive, Henry's army pulled off its share of "rough stuff"; so that it became possible for Frank Murphy, former judge and then mayor of Detroit, to state of his own knowledge: "Henry Ford employs some of the worst gangsters in our city."

The rum-running business was no longer what it had been, for the ring had been so successful in "fixing" the

Federal enforcement service that the job of Henry Ford Shutt became much like ordinary truck-driving, and the pay was reduced accordingly. But it happened that Hank's employer had a brother who was a top man in the Ford "secret section", and asked Hank to get him the "lowdown" on a group of bootleggers who were reported meddling in politics in the town of Dearborn, a pocket borough of Ford's. The information which Hank brought was so useful that for a while he had a double job with double pay; a sort of spy on spies, he came and went through the underworld, and the things he knew would have blown up the political and industrial regime of the Detroit area, if he had not kept them under his own hat and marketed them thriftily. Hank had plenty of money again, and now and then would turn up at the home of his parents and save their lives.

The American people had been told, over a period of many years, that the charitable Mr. Ford made a specialty of giving ex-convicts a chance to rehabilitate themselves; the American people had thought that was a worthy and noble work. But gradually the practices of the Ford Motor Company had changed, until ex-criminals were being hired, not to learn new ways of life, but to go on practicing old ones. This was something of which the American people had yet to learn.

## LXIV

Edsel Ford had four lovely children, three boys and a girl, and these had come to be one of Henry's solaces in life. They were set apart from all other children in the world, because they were going to become the inheritors of this vast empire, they were going to carry on the Ford name and tradition. They were being carefully trained for that responsibility, and would carry it worthily, and justify Henry in his life-long defense of the system of hereditary monarchy in industry. "Democracy has nothing to do with the question who ought to be boss"—so Henry had written in one of his books.

As one of the consequences of the depression there had come a terrifying new development in American life, a wave of kidnapping. Organized bands of gangsters would abduct the children of the rich and hold them for ransom, many times treating them cruelly, more than once killing them when the schemes failed. These happenings became as a great shadow over the life of the Flivver King; he became obsessed with the idea that this horror might befall one of his adored heirs.

The economic aspects of this crime were clear enough to anyone who would stop to think about the matter. The children of the poor played on the streets with entire safety so far as kidnappers were concerned; many parents in those days might have been reconciled to having their little ones carried away, provided they were sure of being fed. But when a man was known to have two hundred millions of cash reserves in the bank, there might be a chance of collecting the biggest ransom in history. The gangsters knew it, and Henry knew that they knew it; so his rest was broken, so love and brotherhood died in his heart, and fear and suspicion grew. Uneasy lies the head that wears a crown.

The man to whom Henry looked for

protection against this danger was Harry Bennett. Bennett would find men who could be trusted to guard the children and not sell out for any number of gangster dollars; they would occupy in the life of the Flivver King the position occupied by the "yeomen of the guard" in England. The head of the service department became commander of the household troops; he came and went at all hours, and was the one who could always "get to" Henry. It often became his task to investigate those who applied for interviews, and sometimes he had the responsibility of deciding whether the request should be granted.

Here again was the billion dollars intervening in Henry's life. Bennett was a man after a billion dollars' own heart; he could hit hard and shoot straight, and was fast on the draw; he was not afraid of anything alive, and to him the right of a billion dollars to rule the world was no more to be disputed than the hardness of steel and the redness of blood. So now he took charge of Henry's life, and the shaping of his mind and character.

The significance of this change becomes apparent when one realizes that the man who had formerly occupied this place in Henry's life was the Reverend Samuel Marquis, sensitive and high-minded Christian gentleman who had given up his job as dean of St. Paul's Cathedral to run Henry's "social department". The billion dollars had been too much for this clergyman; it had made an atmosphere about the Ford plant and the Ford home which he could not breathe. He had resigned and written a book about Henry, in which, with sad but clear insight, he had explained his character. The dean

perhaps did not realize it, but Henry was repeating the story of the dean's own religious system—he was casting out Christ and putting Caesar in his place.

## LXV

Abner Shutt was walking on Fort Street in Detroit; trudging wearily from factory to factory, on chance that some one of them might be "hiring". He had long ago had to part with his flivver; which meant, in that widely spread out area, that he had lost most of his chances of finding a job, or of getting to one if he found it. Whenever he had a carfare he would ride into the city and walk from place to place; if he had the price of a newspaper he would search the advertisements and the news columns in the hope that some concern might be resuming.

He came to a vacant lot with a crowd, and some kind of meeting going on. "Ford Workers Assemble," read a big white streamer; a man standing on the back end of a truck was shouting. Abner still thought of himself as a Ford worker, and stopped to see what they wanted of him.

He listened to a speech by a man who said he had been employed at Ford's for many years. It was the story that Abner knew by heart: the speed-up and the tyranny of the bosses, the senseless petty regulations, the irregularity of employment, the lack of security and the decencies of life. Yes, here was a fellow who knew what he was talking about, and when the crowd shouted, Abner's heart was warmed. Men couldn't talk like that inside the plant, not even in a whisper; but out here America was still free.

The speaker said they were organizing a protest march to Dearborn. They were going to the gates of the plant and tell Henry about the grievances of his workers. Then Abner realized what this was; he had read in the paper that agitators were organizing such a march, and had got permission from the mayor of Detroit to have it. The paper said they were Communists, the notorious and dreaded "Reds". Abner should have heeded this warning, but for the moment he was swept off his feet. The man seemed to be talking workers' talk, and Abner wanted to hear more.

He listened to several speakers, telling not merely about the inside of the plant, which was familiar to him, but many things about Henry Ford's activities in politics, and his refusal to make any contribution to the support of his unemployed workers; about the near bankruptcy of the city of Detroit, and how the bankers, before they would lend another dollar, had forced the city government to turn off hundreds of its employees; they had refused to let the city undertake any new public works and had required the welfare department to cut fifteen thousand destitute families off the relief rolls. Maybe the fathers of some of those families were in this crowd; men shouted that they were.

It was the seventh of March, 1932, and a biting wind was blowing. Men stood shivering and watery-eyed, their ragged coats buttoned tightly, their hands in their pockets. A grey and cloudy day, with snow on the ground; they stamped their feet to warm them. Pitiful, strained faces, dreaming of justice which didn't exist in the world, of freedom to do something more than starve—they were going to present their dreams to the great Lord of Dearborn, who once had been their friend, but now had averted his face from them.

A speaker read their demands, quite a long list: jobs for those who had been laid off, or fifty percent of their wages until they had work again; the slowing of the speed-up, the ending of the spotter system—yes, truly, Ford's would be a pleasanter place to work in if these orators could have their way! "Are you for these demands?" The listeners shouted that they were.

Down the street came an army marching, other ragged and hungry men, assembled at different meetings. They came four abreast, singing an old song, "Solidarity Forever", and carrying banners addressed to the great master. A few policemen walked at their head and alongside; for Mayor Murphy, calling himself a liberal, said that unemployed men should enjoy the right to voice their grievances, and to hold meetings and parades. Everything was to be orderly, the organizers had promised, and the orators warned them that if they committed acts of violence they would forfeit public sympathy, in which lay their one hope.

"We are not armed. We are not rioters, but workers, and American citizens. We present just demands, and assert our right of petition against intolerable wrongs. Stand with us, fellow-workers and comrades!" So the speakers proclaimed, and called upon all who agreed to fall in at the end of the procession. In the distance could be seen the gigantic River Rouge plant, its tall silvered smokestacks rising like a huge pipe-organ. Three thousand out of Henry's hundred and fifty thousand idle men were marching there to tell their troubles; and Abner Shutt was among them.

## LXVI

They came to the city limits of Detroit, where Mayor Murphy's jurisdiction ended. Beyond it was Dearborn, in which the plant lay, a town which Henry ruled; the mayor and all the officials were his. The chief of police was a former Ford policeman, who for years had been paid one salary by Ford and another by the city of Dearborn. He had just got a new supply of machine-guns.

The parade stopped, and the Dearborn police warned them to go no further. An orator answered that they were going to march to the Ford plant and ask to send in a deputation to present their grievances. Again he pledged that it was to be an orderly demonstration, and warned all the paraders accordingly.

The march started, and the police began throwing bombs filled with tear and vomit-gas. But the avenue was wide, and men dodged this way and that, and the march continued. Policemen in cars and on motorcycles rushed ahead to the plant blowing sirens.

Across the avenue Henry had built wide bridges, so that men crossing to his plant would not block traffic. On the first bridge stood his "service men" with gas-bombs and machine-guns. It was an excellent position from the military point of view—provided your enemies were unarmed. A line of Ford police mixed with the Dearborn police were drawn up in front of the gates of the plant. Reporters insisted that there were Detroit police among them—

which looked as if Mayor Murphy was not able to control his own department.

It took some nerve to march up to that position, especially if you were leading, and knew that you were a marked man. Perhaps it was only the fanatical Reds who would dare it; or perhaps it was the other way around—as soon as anyone found the nerve to dare it, they called him a fanatical Red. Anyhow, there they were, the police ordering them to disperse, and they demanding that a delegation be permitted to enter and present their petition.

Abner Shutt was among them, not a little scared, and confused in his thoughts. He had been over that bridge so many times, it seemed like home to him. Wasn't his own son working in there right now? Surely he had a right to ask for a job; surely if Mr. Ford knew about it, he would grant that right! But when Abner saw the men on the bridge throwing bombs at him, and heard them popping around him, he started to back away; when a man by his side clutched at his stomach and collapsed with a bullet through it, Abner turned and ran towards the vacant ground where he had been used to parking his car.

The rest of what happened he did not see, but read about it in the paper. The gates of the plant came open, and Harry Bennett rode out in a car, another man driving, Bennett in the right-hand seat shouting to the crowd to clear the way. Accounts differed as to whether it was a revolver or a gas-pistol he began firing; anyhow, he fired, and some one threw a rock and hit him on the head and sent him to the hospital. Immediately the men on the bridge turned loose a machine-gun into the crowd, and kept up a steady firing until they had wounded about fifty men and killed four.

So there was Henry Ford's answer to Abner Shutt and the rest of his unemployed workers. Or rather, it was the answer of the billion dollars which had taken charge of Henry's life. A score or two of men lay in hospitals with bullet-wounds, also with handcuffs on their wrists and chains fastening them to their beds; but not a single policeman or "service man" had a bullet-wound.

The Ford Model A had gone back to the old days when you could have only one color. It might be called Arabian sand, or Dawn grey, or Niagara blue, or Gun Metal blue—but it would always be Fresh Human Blood.

## LXVII

Abner Shutt rode home alone on the street car, and had a lot of time to think about what had happened. He had been shot at; he had seen a man killed, the first intentional killing he had ever witnessed. He was shocked, and the more he thought about it, the more he was surprised at himself. His habits of order and obedience reasserted themselves, and he said, "I hadn't oughter been there!" He thought about his great and good friend Henry Ford, and how pained he would be by these events, and by Abner's part in them. If Mr. Ford had known the men were coming, he would have talked with them, in the kind and friendly way he had talked with Abner years ago. Why hadn't somebody told him?

These ideas were confirmed when Abner bought the evening paper and read about the leaders of that march being the worst Red agitators there were in the Detroit area. The paper gave their names, which had become familiar to Abner through seeing them in the same paper. So that was it! Those shrewd fellows had succeeded in luring the most loyal of hundred percent Americans, a former klansman, into their trap! Secret agents of the Bolsheviki, who wanted to overthrow this free American government, and make all the workers into slaves like they was in Roossia! Abner was quite sure the workers were slaves in Roossia, having read it in the "Dearborn Independent."

The longer Abner thought about it, the more embarrassed he became. Why, his own son John might have been up there on that bridge, helping to defend the plant against those Communists! His son Hank might have been in the crowd, spotting the enemies of the Ford Motor Company! Abner decided that when he told the family about his adventure, he would vary it slightly; he hadn't marched, but just followed along to see what the agitators would do. The chances were that nobody had recognized him, and what was the use of putting a black mark against his name?

Milly was alarmed by his story, and made him promise he would never again do such a silly thing. Daisy said he might have been the means not merely of getting himself shot, but of getting John and her husband fired, and then where would they be? She had reason enough for these fears; why, they even fired men who raised money for the funerals of those dead marchers!

When Hank showed up a day or

two later, he said that he had been in the crowd and had spotted his father, but had refrained from turning in his name. The old man must sure be getting off his chump to walk into a spot like that.

As a matter of fact Hank hadn't been anywhere near the scene; Daisy had mentioned their father's story over the phone, and Hank's imagination had done the rest. Since he had taken to probing into so many secret affairs, it pleased him to dramatize himself, to see himself everywhere, sharing the confidence of the "big shots", having the real "inside dope" on everybody and everything. So long as Hank kept these "tall tales" for unimportant people like his family, it was all right; he knew better than to try them on his boss.

## LXVIII

In that same month the Ford Motor Company issued two new models of Model A. They did it with the usual fanfare, predicting huge sales and re-employment. But it didn't work that way; it wasn't long before there was a general crash of the banks in Detroit, and more widespread distress than ever. Henry had his own money in those banks, and since he was the only man in the city who had the cash to save them, he had to take them over. So a new principality was added to the Ford empire.

But this did no good to Henry's workers; their jobs had been cut to one or two days a week, and now the minimum wage was reduced to four dollars per day. Economic facts had proven stronger than Henry's theories; but don't imagine that he would change the theories! He still said that the way to prosperity was to pay high wages—he who couldn't pay any wages at all to three-quarters of his men.

This increasing mass of misery pressed upon the people of the Detroit area like a mountain weight. The Shutt family had turned their home into a lodging-house, crowding themselves into two rooms and trying to rent the others. Abner went out and hunted work until his legs gave out, but all he could find was a few small jobs for a meal. He pawned his watch, then his overcoat; that was all right in summer, but now it was fall, and he had to beg Hank for the means of redeeming his coat.

Milly was bedridden most of the time, and they no longer had money for a doctor. The last one had prescribed medicine, but she couldn't afford to go on taking it, and anyhow it hadn't seemed to do her much good. Daisy had to run the house, and she too was complaining. She had tried desperately to keep from having a baby, and had had two abortions; but the last one had made her so ill that she hadn't dared to have another, so now she had a baby whom she didn't much care for, and he was rather spindling because she hadn't much milk. She had become a household drudge, and so much of a slattern that her virtue was safe from the lodgers most of the time.

Such bright dreams she had had, of being an elegant stenographer in an office, wearing silk stockings, and perhaps having a chance to marry a boss. Instead she had got a poor clerk who had only one or two days a week at the new four-dollar minimum; they had transferred him to the payroll department, but the payroll had been cut

to about one-tenth of normal. Jim
Baggs was his name, and he liked to
go to ball-games and shout at the players, and also he was fond of bowling;
but now he had no money for any sort
of amusement, and his wife had lost
interest in him.

That was the way the depression
broke the lives of the poor and those
whom it made poor. In Detroit were
tens of thousands of homeless men,
sleeping in the parks, digging themselves holes in sandpiles, sitting all day
at the docks hoping to catch a fish.
And then in the newspapers you read
the clamor of the rich that the governments of the city and the state must
"economize"; by which they meant re-
ducing relief expenditures and throwing more people off the rolls, without
giving them the least idea what to do.
In their town of Highland Park the
Shutts couldn't get relief because they
owned a home; but what were they
supposed to do with that home, sit in
it and freeze to death, or starve, or
both? They couldn't sell it for anything.

When you presented this argument
to the relief people, they answered that
the town was near bankruptcy, and
there was no more money; if they increased the taxes it wouldn't mean that
the city got extra money, but merely
that more people would give up their
homes and apply for relief, and what
good would that do? No member of
the Shutt family knew the answer to
such riddles, and if anybody in the
whole world knew, how was that magical person to be recognized?

Another presidential election was
coming, and perhaps they might learn
through that. The Republicans re-

nominated the Great Engineer; to do
otherwise would be to acknowledge
failure, and besides they were satisfied
with what he had done, giving government credit to the rich, from whom
prosperity would have to flow whenever it got ready to flow again. The
Democrats nominated the governor of
New York State, and he began making eloquent speeches over the radio,
promising to try a New Deal; but the
Shutts had had to sell their radio, and
got their campaign news through the
papers, which assured them that economic laws could not be repealed by
political speeches.

The great and good Henry Ford issued a statement to all the workers in
his plant advising them to vote for
President Hoover. Abner still thought
of himself as a Ford worker, but he
didn't need the advice, being used to
resisting the blandishments of Democratic orators. Daisy and her Jim
were so embittered by their situation
that they declared they were going to
vote for Roosevelt. Before the campaign was over they got wrought up
about it, and kept arguing with the
old man. But Abner had learned to
shut up and keep his thoughts to himself, and he did it now; he proved himself a free and independent American
by voting for Hoover.

## LXIX

Daisy Baggs had been, in happier
days, a movie fan. Now she no longer
had the price, but she had managed to
find a substitute anodyne. On the avenue was a candy-store where they sold
odds and ends, including old magazines; you could buy much worn cop-

ies of what were called "the pulps" for as low as five cents a copy, and get half the money back when you returned them. That was cheap enough happiness for the poorest of starved souls. Daisy would devour these magazines in her spare hours, and would read them aloud to her mother.

They were always "romances", and invariably they dealt with rich and happy and successful people—at least they were that at the end of the story, which made it different from real life, and explained why poor and lonely and unsuccessful people paid their pennies for them. In these stories poor girls who studied hard and became stenographers did really marry the boss, and not just some bookkeeper on part time. Girls in lodging houses married rich miners, or men with hearts of gold who soon afterwards struck oil. Handsome but poor boys would stop a runaway horse and so meet and marry the greatest of heiresses; or perhaps they would save the life of a "magnate", and be invited to his home.

Abner used to hear these stories when he sat at home resting his tired legs. They gave him new ideas about how to succeed in life; but unfortunately he was no longer young or handsome, and opportunity seemed to have passed him by. The one rich man upon whom his thoughts were centered had never been known to ride a horse, and never got into any trouble or danger so far as Abner knew. Mr. Ford had great numbers of people surrounding him, and presumably ready to do for him whatever he needed. Abner had seen him a few times, when he walked through the plant, or was driven out of it by his chauffeur; but there never had been any occasion when Abner could speak to him. Abner had learned where his home was, and had driven past the place, and knew that there were men on guard, and that one did not just drive in. No, the good old days were by, when a workingman could talk to Henry Ford and tell him anything or ask him a favor.

However, the stories which Daisy read and talked about had the effect of keeping in Abner's mind the idea of a bridge between master and worker. Abner too began dreaming romances; making up stories of what might happen. Suppose he should step out of the assembly line when Henry was passing, and say: "Mr. Ford, I am Abner Shutt, who helped to lift your gasoline buggy out of a mudhole nearly forty years ago." Or that he should call at Mr. Ford's home and tell that story to the guard; or wait on the three thousand acre farm—the great man must walk over it some time, and he couldn't have it all fenced in!

Or suppose Abner wrote a letter. The papers said that Mr. Ford got thousands of letters every day, but it might be that even a secretary had a heart, and could be touched by a tragic story such as Abner had to tell. Each writer of a begging letter has the same fond idea; each is a separate individual, a drop of water falling from the sky; but presently the drops find they have become part of a river, and are on their way to an ocean!

One day it chanced that Abner came home to find Daisy out and his wife asleep; and that was what he wanted—a chance to have his own way without having to answer questions. Secretiveness had come to be one of his qualities, owing to living in the house with so many people who didn't agree with him about this and that, and called him stingy, or a mossback, or whatever it was that young people were saying about the old. Abner Shutt was not clever, but he had figured out for himself that it was better for a workingman's letter to look like what it was, than to be written in the business college script of his educated daughter.

In the paper Abner had read something about the charitableness of Mrs. Ford, and her activities in church work; he had figured out that maybe she didn't get so many letters as her husband. He found a pen and ink, and tore a sheet of paper out of a notebook, and with more labor and sweat than he had ever expended on the assembly line he composed a letter, beginning "Dear Misses Ford," and continuing:

"Wen I was a kid I usto live in back of Bagly st and many times I help lifft the buggy outa the mud and onst to turn her rownd. I workt in the Mack av place sinse the companys first yeer. I talked sometimes with mister Ford in them days. I workt for him near thirty years and always good. I ben layed off now two yeers, I got a sick wife, and my dawta has got a baby, her huzban has got one day weak in the offise. My son has ben thru mister Fords trade scool, he has got a famly and only two days weak. Mister Ford knoes my name he give me a job hissef he talk to me many a time. Misses Ford please get me a job I do annything I know the Ford car I

work by it all my life. Pleas help a good man I belong Rev Orguts church. Yr respy Abner Shutt."

## LXX

Abner read this letter over and had an uneasy feeling that some of the words didn't look quite right. But he reflected that he wasn't applying for a job as a school teacher. He thought that "Misses Ford" would be able to make out what the letter was about, and in this he was correct. He made only one serious mistake; he forgot to put any address on the letter.

He went out and bought a stamp and mailed it, and then sat down to wait. He did not tell any of the family; he would surprise them. He waited at the house all the next day, expecting some messenger to come. He waited all the following day; until Milly and Daisy began to scold—had he given up altogether the idea of looking for work? He went out to walk the streets again.

What happened to the letter was that one of Mrs. Ford's secretaries opened it, and marked it for investigation, as Mrs. Ford had directed in such cases. It was forwarded to an official in the administration building who attended to these matters. The man looked up the name of Abner Shutt in the card-file containing several million names of the former employees of the Ford Motor Company. The lack of address wasn't so important, for the reason that Abner Shutt was not a very common name. The records showed that he had been with the company as he stated; and so the case was referred to a "field worker".

A young man alighted from his Ford Model A "coop" in front of the Shutt home and rang the bell. He stood there quite a while, ringing, because there was no one at home but Milly, who rarely got up. But at last she came tottering to the door and peered through the crack, and was, of course, much flustered when she saw a strange man who said he was from the company. Stammering apologies, Milly let him in, and then sat down groaning, and at the same time distressed because of the poverty of her home, its unfitness as a place of reception.

It was a sad fact that many of the "sob-stories" which came in the mail to the kind Mrs. Ford were frauds. But in this case the investigator could see that Milly really was sick, and it became apparent that she didn't know that her husband had written the letter. That made it easy to check the truth of everything Abner had told. The husband was out looking for work, it appeared; an honorable if futile procedure. The young man asked questions covering every detail of the family and financial affairs of the Shutts. Unlikely as it seemed, the man apparently had known Mr. Ford in his early days, and had been personally hired by him and promoted by him. It was a case for attention.

What excitement in the Shutt family when its members came home one by one and heard that story! And how proud of himself was the head of the household! Long idleness and helplessness had all but broken his spirit; but now his crest rose, it was hard to live in the house with him. He waited each day for the postman, and finally received a notice to report at the Highland Park plant, where they were still making parts for the old Model Ts. Abner was going to insert some small screws on the magneto assembly line two days each week, and for that he would have eight dollars and no carfare to pay. It sounded like heaven to people who had been so near to starving.

When a man has twenty-five thousand employees, it really will not bankrupt him to make it twenty-five thousand and one; especially as he is free to fire some other man, or a hundred others if he thinks best. The point is that a man wants his wife to be happy, and if she has a tender heart, that is to be expected in women, who find it so hard to understand economic laws. If a wife refuses to order her begging letters destroyed unread, there has to be a way to satisfy her wishes. So Abner Shutt got a job, and wrote a letter of touching gratitude, quite convincing as to its scrawl and spelling; it was put before the great lady, and she carried it in her handbag and showed it to some of her friends, so that they might know what a good and kind institution the Ford Motor Company was.

As for Abner, he forgot all his wounds and grievances overnight. He forgot the bullets which had whistled by his head—bullets purchased on Henry Ford's account and aimed by men in his employ. Let that secret of Abner's be locked away and never mentioned while he lived. Abner knew again what he had always known in his heart, that Henry Ford was one of the greatest and best of men, and that if anything went wrong it was because his business was so big, and he could not find men worthy of his purposes. Now again Abner Shutt was one of the insiders, and if ever any boss or underling dared to fire him, he would know what to do!

## LXXI

In spite of Henry's urging, the American people did not re-elect President Hoover. They took a chance on the Democrat; and almost at once there began a breakdown of finance and industry, the worst yet experienced. The learned ones fell to arguing, and would continue to do so throughout the rest of American history: was it the result of what Mr. Hoover had done or failed to do, or was it because of the people's fear of what Mr. Roosevelt meant to do? The President invited the President-elect to consult with him as to what should be done prior to the inauguration; but Mr. Roosevelt declined to assume any responsibility for anything that might be done during Mr. Hoover's term. So there was more controversy. Who was to blame for all the banks of the country having to close?

Abner was one of a hundred million Americans who only knew what they read in the papers. To him it was all utterly mysterious and beyond comprehending. What was going to become of the country? Was it going all to pot? Was Ford's going to have to close down again and cost him his job?

The new President kept cheerful and smiling, which helped some people mightily, and enfuriated others. The new President had the general idea that if you gave money to the farmers and workers of the country they would put it into circulation right away; instead of giving it to the big banks to keep hidden in their vaults. This new plan sounded fine to all the people who didn't have any money, and their promises to spend it were hearty and sincere. The plan was tried, and straightway goods began to be bought, and industry began to pick up; the farmers had a market for their products, and the plain people had food to put into their stomachs.

That was the story of the next few years. The government borrowed billions of dollars, and by one device or another gave it or loaned it to people who would spend it, and they did, and so the banks and the big business men had the fun of making it all over again. One would have thought this was what they wanted, and that they would have been grateful to the President who had thought up this smart idea and got it going; but for some strange reason, no sooner were they safe again, the banks open and stuffed with money, the farmers getting good prices and the corporations paying the biggest dividends in their history, than they all began to turn against the man who had saved them, to call him a dictator and spendthrift, and other things too bad to print.

Take Henry Ford, for example: towards the end of 1934, after a year and a half of the New Deal, Henry came out with a public announcement that the depression was over, and that he was scheduling a million cars, the most he had made since 1930. And it really was true this time, not just psychology. The people had money to replace the old cars they had been driving for years, and Henry began calling back his workers and raising his minimum wage. Wouldn't one expect him to make some change in his economic philosophy, and some effort to co-operate with this new administration?

But no! The administration tried to establish a thing called the N.R.A., which would compel manufacturers to abolish wage-cutting and blind over-production, and all the wastes of anarchy in industry; and Henry, most stubborn of individualists, took his stand like a mule in the middle of the road, refusing to sign up, refusing to say what he would do, leaving it to the government to boycott his car and refuse to consider his bids.

What was Abner Shutt to make of events like that? The answer was that Abner made nothing of them whatever. Abner resembled another mule in industry, one that was hitched to a pole, and set to walking round and round, turning a piece of machinery. So many times per hour he made the circle, and kept it up for eight hours a day, five days of the week, and asked nothing in all the world but to be hitched like that for as long as he was able to walk; so that every Friday evening he might have one of the Ford Motor Company's good checks, and be able to feed and clothe his family, and pay the taxes on his home, and perhaps get a few dollars in the bank—this time under government guarantee—so that if another of those economic cyclones should hit the country he and his sick wife would not be blown away.

## LXXII

At this time another member of the family got his name into the newspapers. There was a group of students at the University who objected to military training, and they called a meeting in opposition to "War and Fascism," and made it picturesque by holding a mock trial and burning William Randolph Hearst in effigy. This made a stir in the newspapers, and the president of the university felt it necessary to announce that no more such disturbances of the peace of War and Fascism would be permitted. The trouble had been caused, he said, "by the pervasive activity of a few professional agitators." The newspapers mentioned several students who were involved, among them a member of the senior class by the name of Thomas Shutt.

Abner had ceased to be an attentive reader of the papers, and the first he knew about the matter was when a delegation of three citizens came to call on him. They were old acquaintances who had worn the hat-bands of the "Highland Park Ford for President Club", and had ridden with Abner to the burning of a fiery cross. The activities of the Klan had lapsed, and the tired old worker had lost interest in political affairs; but these visitors told him that he was neglecting his duties as a citizen, and that he should have licked the tar out of that kid rather than let the Reds get hold of him.

Poor Abner Shutt was distressed, and assured the men very earnestly that he hadn't known a thing about it. Hiding deep in his heart the guilt of once having marched in a Red parade, he declared that he was just as good and loyal a patriot as ever; but how could he keep track of his son when he didn't understand what the boy was studying?—"all them highbrow words he uses," said Abner. And what could he do now, when the kid had grown up to be a football player, strong enough to lick two of his father?

The visitors said they would come and help administer the licking, if necessary. They warned Abner solemnly that there was a new organization, even stronger than the Klan, having the backing of many of the big companies, and out to see to it that the Detroit area did not fall into the hands of no Red bastards. They wouldn't tell him much about it, because he could no longer be trusted, but they dropped terrifying hints, and caused the poor old man to write a letter to his son—a badly confused one, which filled Tom's heart with pity, but did not change his ideas.

The father kept hearing about this new vigilante group, the Black Legion, which was building up a great membership, especially among the "hillbillies", the white workers of the South whom the motor companies were now recruiting and bringing in by the tens of thousands every season. These men were mostly illiterate, but they were patriotic, and full of racial pride; they hated Catholics, Jews, Negroes, and anybody who could be called a "Red". One of them worked in the Highland Park plant with Abner and rode home with him often, and couldn't keep from dropping hints about this new society, even though he had sworn with a pistol at his head never to reveal its secrets.

A most terrifying affair, that "Black Oath" which you had to sign with your blood. "I do swear in the name of God and the Devil to devote my life to the obedience of my superiors, and to exert every means in my power for the extermination of the anarchist, the

Communist, the Roman hierarchy and their abettors." You had to be a "native-born white Protestant Gentile American citizen", and to accept the punishment of death for failure to keep your oath; you would be "torn limb from limb and be scattered to the carrion." You put on a black robe and went out and inflicted the penalties of "fire, flogging, and death" upon the enemies of your ideas.

This order was building a tremendous political power; the leaders were judges, prosecutors, mayors, councilmen, policemen, militiamen, and members of the American Legion. Poor Abner hadn't sworn any oath, but he was in great fear because of the activities of his wayward son. What a mistake to let the boy go to college, and pick up dangerous notions, and learn to use all them highbrow words!

Things were growing more tense every day; even poor dull and wearied Abner had to perceive it. In Dearborn, in which city the River Rouge plant lay, the Ford people had organized another group, called the Knights of Dearborn, comprised of several hundred men on the Ford payroll who did political work and pulled off whatever "rough stuff" might be needed. A sort of mania of spying was spreading inside Henry's plant. Three men standing together talking were enough to constitute a conspiracy. The service men searched the lunch-boxes of the workers for seditious literature. They even pried open sandwiches in the search!

## LXXIII

Tom Shutt came out of college. He came in a black cap and gown and a blaze of glory; lovely class singing on warm spring evenings, swarms of pretty girls in soft alluring costumes, mothers and fathers all handsome and elegant, and a famous lawyer delivering the baccalaureate, telling a thousand young men and women going out into life that America needed their idealism and high devotion at a time when forces of discontent and disorder were loose in the world.

Only one member of the Shutt family was free to witness this great occasion in the life of its youngest member, and that was Daisy Baggs. She wasn't sure if she ought to come among such fashionable people, but Tom had invited her, so she paid a neighbor to look after her baby, and borrowed a dress from a friend who was a manicurist. Also she borrowed the family flivver, motored the thirty miles or so to Ann Arbor, and parked the dingy object a long way from the campus.

She was awe-stricken by all the elegance and splendor; it was like being taken into the fair world of the "pulps". Her brother looked so grand she could hardly believe he was the same kid whose nose she used to wipe. He introduced her to a lovely co-ed in pale blue chiffon, the daughter of a manufacturer, who gazed upon him with what appeared to be doglike devotion; so Daisy understood the meaning of a college education. She was so impressed that she conceived a great act of renunciation, worthy of one of her fiction heroines; she would steal away and not spoil this occasion by making Tom introduce his poor ignorant sister to his rich and learned friends.

But Tom would not have it so. He was going back home, he said, and asked her to wait till night and drive him and his suitcases. During the hour of the ride he did his best to shatter her romantic dreams. College was "the bunk"; the cap and gown had been hired for two dollars, and the great lawyer whose eloquent idealism had so moved her was a hireling of the power corporations to help them to control the Republican party and choose the state legislators and judges. If he had dealt with truth in his baccalaureate he would have told the thousand young people that they were a superfluous generation, and that unless papa found them a job they were sunk before they sailed.

As for the lovely daughter of the manufacturer, she was a good enough kid, but Tom hadn't asked her to marry him because she didn't understand his point of view and he wasn't going to settle down as anybody's house-pet. The girl he might hit it off with was that cute little one with large spectacles and slightly stooped shoulders; she had got that way bending over a study-table preparing a set of graphs showing the relationship of profits and wages in depressions throughout American history. Real wages always dropped quicker than profits, she had proved, and they never came back so fast. Those graphs covered the troubles of the Shutt family during several generations.

It was close to midnight; part of a moon was rising in front of them, and flower-scents on the breeze; the highway bright with the lights of cars returning to Detroit—everything lovely, and poor Daisy yearning to hear something happy and inspiring out of that fashionable college world! Instead, here was a young man with no illusions, except possibly as to his own strength and determination; he was going into life with his teeth set in a mood of battle.

"Tom, you talk like a Red!" exclaimed his sister.

"Maybe the newspapers will call me one," he answered. "Long before I went to college I'd made up my mind that labor was getting a crooked deal, and what I've got out of my four years' study are the facts and figures to prove it."

### LXXIV

"And what are you going to do next, Tom?" was Daisy's question; and the answer was:

"I'm going to get me a job at Ford's and earn some money."

"You mean as a worker?"

"Sure, that's what I mean."

To Daisy it was a blow over the precise spot where romantic dreams are generated. Four years of high school and four more of college—and at the end of it all to go on the belt! "What was the use of getting an education, Tom, if you don't mean to use it?"

"Oh, I'll use it all right," said he. "I'll be a worker that knows what's happening to him; and maybe I can tell some of the others."

"You're going to be a trouble-maker?"

"I'll be called that, Sis. Will it worry you?"

"It won't be so good for the rest of us."

"Have things been so awful good of late?"

"They were just starting to look good again."

Tom laughed. "If you'd rather I worked elsewhere, I'll move along. America is a big country."

"Oh, I wouldn't say that! But it'll be hard for Mom and Pop to understand. We all thought you were going to study law."

"Well, Sis, I learned there were a hundred lawyers on relief in Detroit, and I thought that was enough. I'd rather take my chance on the belt."

Daisy was silent for a bit, then she said: "If I was you I wouldn't talk to the family about my ideas or what I meant to do. They won't understand, and it'll only make them unhappy. Just say you're getting a job for the summer, while you take time to look around."

"All right, Sis, you know them better than I."

"And something else: don't talk to Hank about yourself at all."

"What's it about Hank?"

"I haven't the right to talk about his affairs, Tom."

"Not to a member of the family?"

"If he chooses to talk, that's up to him. I won't tell you about him and I won't tell him about you."

"Humph!" said Tom. "I suppose prohibition repeal has knocked Hank's business."

"You'll have to do your own guessing about that."

"Most of those birds have settled down to running beer-parlors, I'm told. Wouldn't anybody take Hank on?"

"He's got the habit of roaming round. I don't think he'd be satisfied pushing a cash register."

"He's doing some sort of stool-pigeon work, eh?"

"It's not fair to ask me questions, Tom."

"All right, I won't. But as it happens, I know that Ford's is a nest of spying. It'll be amusing if I run into my own brother. He might be spying on me, and again I might be spying on him. How about it, Sis?"

"Mom's feeling pretty low," said Daisy, "and I don't think she's going to be with us much longer. Something the matter with her that the doctors can't find out about."

## LXXV

Everybody said it was nice to have Tom back in his old home. They were disposed to be in awe of him, because of the vast learning he had acquired, but he did not put on any "dog" with his family or their friends. He was the same kind fellow he had always been; as a boarder he was the best, because he brought his money home promptly, and more than he had to.

He went right out and got himself a job at Ford's. That was the advantage of being young and husky, and knowing how to talk to people. Many college boys came to the gates of factories in the latter part of the month of June, looking for a chance to earn their keep over the summer and their tuition for the winter, and many bosses had come to realize that they were full of energy and not afraid to expend it. Tom's generation of students was not so entirely "superfluous," after all; as a result of having spent eight years on higher education, he would be able to get preference over veteran laborers for the digging of ditches or the loading of cement sacks into freight cars; also in a host of new jobs which modern industry had created, requiring what is called "personality"; the filling of motor-car tanks and wiping of windshields, the escorting of passengers into aeroplanes, the demonstrating of elec-

tric refrigerators, the giving of lectures on the operation of gadgets—all kinds of activities aided by putting on smart uniforms and manifesting enthusiasm and charm.

They put Tom Shutt at work on pinion gears. Before the depression one man had tended four machines. There had been no change in the machines, but now they required one man to tend twelve, and the last man had played out. It took just about ten minutes to show the job, and that was all Tom would ever need to know about the automobile industry. He would trot up and down the row of machines, stopping at each to take out a completed piece of steel and put in an incompleted one. He didn't mind it a bit, he insisted; it left him free to think about the things he was interested in, and at the end of every Friday he had earned five times five dollars and sixty-five cents. Tom wanted it to last forever; but something told him it wouldn't.

He got himself a light car on instalments; a Ford, of course—it wouldn't do to park any other kind in the huge lot reserved for Ford workers. The company always denied that it enforced any such rule, but if anyone would have the nerve to park a "chevvy" in that lot, it wouldn't be many hours before the boss would find something wrong with his work. Tom didn't want to give any sort of offense to anybody; he was diligent, and as mild as a lamb; did what he was told, and studied the regulations as he had formerly studied the relation of wages to profits in his economics class.

His idea was to get to know his fellow workers; but that didn't come about so naturally as one might have supposed. The men came in a hurry in the morning, punched the time-clock, threw off their coats, and went to work. There wasn't much time for chatting when you had to get your lunch, stuff it in, wipe your hands, and be on the job in precisely fifteen minutes. After work you bolted to your flivver or to the street car and went to your home, which might be anywhere within a radius of fifty square miles.

But somehow Tom managed it; and when he got to know a man he fell to talking about what had happened to him and to others, and whether there was anything wrong about it, and if so, what. It wasn't long before Tom had discussed these questions with scores of men; and presently, without his having done anything special about it, groups of men were meeting quietly in one another's homes at night, talking about what interested them most.

## LXXVI

In many colleges there were groups of young people concerned about these problems of industry; little "brain trusts", you might call them, and when they came out of college, they seemed to have ways of getting into contact with one another. They didn't all agree in their ideas; on the contrary they wasted an immense amount of time arguing about tactics. But they could get together on what they called "immediate aims", and one of these was to make personal contacts with the workers, and find out what they were thinking, and perhaps suggest new thoughts to them. For this reason many of the students, both men and women, were doing the same as Tom Shutt; getting real jobs, and earning real money, and at the same time putting themselves in position to join a union of workers, if and when such a thing might come into being.

To these little "brain trusts" it seemed plain that the great amount of unemployment in the country was due to lack of spending power in the hands of the masses. Too large a share of the product of industry went to the owners, who spent it in new investments, rather than to the workers, who could have spent it for food and clothing and other needs. The wages of the workers wouldn't buy their product, and so production slowed down, and wages fell still lower, and the farmers had no market for their wheat and corn. The shoe factories were on half-time because the automobile workers were wearing old shoes—so it went, in a series of vicious circles.

The worst of it was that the remedies which the New Deal was applying were not meeting the trouble. Government borrowing and spending caused industry to revive, but left nearly as many unemployed as before. Tom's friends could see it any day at Ford's, where every department was putting in new machines and speeding up the old ones, forcing a smaller number of workers to produce the extra amount of goods. Production had come back to pre-depression levels with only two-thirds of the former number of workers. So it appeared that ten million unemployed were to be a permanent feature of American life; and of course they would always be at the factory gates, beating down wages of the others.

The big "brain trust" in Washington had tried to solve this problem by an invention called the N.R.A., to fix wages and prices. But the Supreme Court had just thrown it out, and that was that. Now the little "brain trusts" in Highland Park and Dearborn and thousands of other industrial centers were saying: "We've got to do it ourselves." Tom Shutt was saying: "We've got to have a union of the automobile workers; a mass union, that means business, not just a bunch of officials warming the seats of swivel chairs and drawing fat salaries."

Here in the Detroit area a start had already been made. There was a group called the Mechanics' Educational Society started during the height of the depression. Its leaders were the tool and die men, the most highly skilled workers, and the ones of whom the bosses stood in fear. They had pulled several quick strikes and won them. More important yet, they had spread their ideas, and set all the auto workers to thinking and talking.

There was a new stirring in labor all over the country; a demand for unions organized according to industries and not according to crafts. It was an old idea, which had had to wait for the workers to realize the need. In the midst of mass poverty and mass unemployment thousands of workers in the Detroit area had started discussing this fundamental idea, that there must be one big union of workers in the motor-car industry, regardless of what kind of work they did. Henry Ford, master of the labor of two hundred thousand men, would deal with one union of that number, and not with a hundred small unions.

## LXXVII

All that summer Tom Shutt kept his job and saved a part of his money. The motor-car industry continued to pick up, and there was full time for all the men of the family. Daisy stayed home and kept the house, for her mother was helpless—it had turned out that her illness was cancer of the stomach, and she suffered a great deal and made things hard for them all. Before the end of the year she was out of her misery, and they had the money to give her a decent burial.

Abner continued to put in his five full days on the magneto assembly line. Prices kept going up, but he was content, remembering past troubles and not having them any more. He was proud of his son who had been through college, even though distressed about his radical ideas. Tom never tried to argue with him. Let him come home and enjoy the peace he had earned; fix up the fences, potter with the chickens, play with his grandson, or sit on the front steps and smoke his pipe. For forty-two years he had earned his way, and produced many times as much as he got; but it was too late for him to try to catch up.

The John Crock Shutts also were on their way up again. The motor-car industry was coming back with a rush, and it restored John to the class of those who were paid by the month. The couple were buying a home again, but this time a more modest one. What they had got out of the depression was a dreadful scare, and the grimmest determination never to be caught again. When the next slump arrived, John was going to have so much skill and Annabelle so many influential friends that they would be safe on top of the heap. They had become ravenous for success; worshipping the Ford machine and everybody in it with such fervor that they were intolerable to their youngest brother.

This feeling was mutual. John and Annabelle thought that Tom was "high-hatting" them, because he had a college education and a number of highbrow friends. Annabelle snorted that her husband, who hadn't bothered with cultural frills, had risen higher than Tom ever had or would. She read about the "brain trust" in the newspapers, and hated those young snobs who were amusing themselves turning the country's business upside down. She referred to her brother-in-law as a "sorehead", and took pains to tell all her friends that they had no responsibility for him, not the slightest, never saw him, scarcely even knew him.

Annabelle was a tight-lipped and sharp-spoken young matron, who managed her two children firmly, stood no nonsense from her maid, and carried the same martinet attitude into her utterances on political and social questions. She wanted labor agitation put down promptly, before it got out of hand, and she took its continuance as a personal affront to herself.

A great empire like Ford's has that effect upon those who live in it and by it. It develops its own needs, and its own loyalties to meet them. Its courtiers and servitors may quarrel furiously among themselves, but they must accept the basic standards upon which the great structure rests. If it is a commercial empire, they must believe in money, and the symbols of money, its codes of excellence and elegance. The Flivver King himself had handed down the law, from the high mountain where he dwelt: "Men work for money." And John and Annabelle did so.

## LXXVIII

Strange as it might seem, Hank Shutt's attitude towards his youngest brother was very much the same. Hank had gone and made himself respectable—and don't think that he hadn't felt it being an outlaw, don't think he hadn't known it when the members of his family were looking down on him, ashamed to mention his name even while they were obliged to take his money! Here he had got himself on the side of law and order, got the powerful Ford organization behind him, and now came this kid brother to risk spoiling it all—this young fool with his head stuffed full of notions by a lot of theoretical people that had never done a day's real work in their lives, and had no idea of the criminals there were among the working classes, and the dangers of stirring them up to violence.

There had been antagonism between these two brothers since childhood. Hank, four years the older, would naturally have been looked up to by Tom; but the younger could not recall a time when he hadn't known that Hank would cheat at games, and tell lies to get himself out of scrapes. Gradually Tom had learned to choose his own crowd. Now here they were a score of years later, in the same situation, each with his own crowd, and the only trouble was that the two crowds were going to war.

Hank came to see his sister about it. He was getting into a jam, he said, and Daisy would have to talk to that crazy kid. She asked why he didn't do it himself, and he said that he couldn't afford to. "I can't go advertisin' a business like mine."

"I think Tom has guessed it pretty well," said Daisy.

"It's one thing to let him guess, and another to be able to say I told him. I just can't afford to talk to no union agitator."

"Can you afford to let me admit it to him?"

"It's a hell of a mess!" burst out Hank. "Am I goin' to turn in my own brother?"

"You have to suit yourself, Hank."

"Sooner or later the boss is bound to find out about him; and then he says to me, 'What the hell? You workin' for both sides, or what is it?' You know there's nothin' the unions would like better than to have a line into the Ford service department."

"Of course, Hank. I see your point of view all right. But you have to see Tom's. It puts him on the spot too. There's nothing the Ford service department would like better than to have a line into the unions. No doubt they've got more than one."

"I ain't sayin' what they got," said Hank, glumly.

"I'm not asking, and Tom's not telling me. I'm just pointing out what he will say when I talk to him. It's as hard for him to explain to his union friends as it is for you to explain to your boss."

"I was at this work before he come along," growled Hank.

"Maybe so, but you didn't tell him. As a matter of fact, he offered to go somewhere else, if the family didn't want him."

"Lissen, Dais', that's the way out o' this mess right now. Can't you get him to move on to some other place? Let him get a job with G.M. I'll stake him while he makes the shift. Tell him it's worth a hundred bucks to me—you can raise it to two hundred if you think that stands in the way. It'd sure be a load off my mind."

So Daisy went to Tom, who laughed and said that Hank had come too late, he had enlisted for the war, and couldn't desert his friends. If there was any money to be paid, let Hank be the lucky one. Tom thought he knew where a hundred bucks could be raised now and then, if Hank would bring in news about the Ford service department, and especially the stool-pigeons they had among the "agitators."

Hank turned pale when he heard that proposition. "Don't you see how I'm on the spot? The very thing that'll be in the boss's mind. How'll I manage to persuade him I didn't fall for it?"

"You don't think you'll fall for it, Hank?"

"How long would I be allowed to live if I started on that racket? It's somethin' they just don't let you do."

"I'll say no more about it," said Daisy. "You don't have to worry about that."

"But it leaves me just where I started. What'm I goin' to do about Tom?"

"I asked him, and he said, do your duty."

Daisy said it with a trace of a smile, but Hank was in no such mood. "A fine thing, I gotta go to the boss and say my own brother's a Red?"

"It ought to help you with him."

"I don't like these melodrama stunts, it takes too damn much explainin'." After a moment he added: "And besides, I don't like to hurt the kid."

"I don't think you need worry about that, Hank. It won't worry Tom to get fired."

"I tell you the kid's life's in danger, Dais'!"

"He knows it," replied the sister, quietly.

"Playin' for martyrdom, hey? Wants some cheap notoriety. Goddam soreheads—Red bastards"—Hank started on a spell of name-calling, until his sister said: "Don't take it too seriously, kiddo. Remember, you're only Henry Ford Shutt, you're not Henry Ford!"

## LXXIX

In midwinter, with heavy snow on the ground, there was a thaw, and then an overnight freeze, and Tom, driving to his work in the morning, skidded into another car, and when the two were disentangled, it was found he had a bent front axle, and had to get a tow-car and be hauled in for repairs. As a result, he was more than an hour late for his work, and when he got onto the floor another man was tending his machines.

That was to be expected, of course; he was due to be docked heavily. But when he started to explain to the boss, he saw it was more than that. "It's all right, Shutt," said the man. "I've had enough trouble from you. Go and get your time."

"What other trouble have you ever had from me?" demanded Tom.

"I don't want any words with you.

There's another man on your job. Get out."

Tom glanced about. A lot of the men in this part of the shop knew him, and he thought of the possibility of trying to call them out. Many a strike had started that way, and been won. But two huskies in plain clothes came strolling along. You could always tell the service men by their broken noses and cauliflower ears. One of them had his right hand in his pocket, which probably meant "brass knucks". It was all a man's life was worth to make a disturbance in that place.

"All right," said Tom, quietly, and turned and went to the room where the men kept their hats and coats. The two secret section men followed him, and saw that he got his time and gave up his badge, and left the plant by the nearest gate.

So Tom had the "martyrdom" he had asked for; he was now a black-listed Ford worker, which meant that he could not work for any big industry in the Detroit area under his own name. They would ask the last place he had worked, and a telephone call would finish his chances. The new boss would seldom say, "We don't want any agitators in this shop." No, for there was now an agitator in the White House, and a lot more of them in Congress, and they were passing fool laws making it hard for business men to protect themselves. The boss would say, politely, "Sorry, buddy, but the fellow that used to have this job has showed up, and we try to keep our old men as much as we can."

Tom had money saved up for just this emergency, and was now free to lead the life of a labor organizer. In the daytime he attended committee meetings, and met with men of the night shifts in the various plants; in the evenings he met the daytime workers, or spoke at meetings, which were held in obscure halls in working class districts. The workers came by devious routes, parked their aged cars a long way off, and stole into the halls by back entrances, or with their caps pulled low and handkerchiefs over their faces. The meetings were held in absolute darkness, and several husky workers stood by the switches to make sure that no one sneaked up on them. That was the way matters stood in all the automobile towns, the steel and rubber and oil towns of this land of the free and home of the brave; the effort of men to meet and discuss their grievances among themselves was a semicriminal activity, in which one engaged not merely at peril of his job, but of his life and limb.

## LXXX

That co-ed whom Tom Shutt had described to his sister as "the cute little one with large spectacles and slightly stooped shoulders" had come to Detroit and got herself a job with the city's welfare department. Her name was Dell Brace, and she was a conscientious young woman who had plunged herself up to the neck in the cause of the workers. Her father was a state senator in Iowa, a reactionary Republican who considered his daughter a victim of the treasonable propaganda in the colleges. That explained why Dell wanted her job anywhere but in the hog and corn belt. The reason for Detroit was that she and Tom had been talking for some time about getting married.

Just as she got her job, he lost his, and he took up a sudden notion about his dignity and declared that he wouldn't let his wife support him; whereupon the tears welled up in the young thing's eyes, and she accused him of going "bourgeois" on her. Did he believe in his principles or didn't he? If a woman was the equal of a man, why shouldn't she be as free to support him as to be supported by him? Tommy, who couldn't bear to see a woman cry, gave way and said all right, and they settled the matter by going that afternoon and getting a license.

So here he was, bringing his bride home to meet the family; and Daisy, awe-stricken by this collegiate young lady, but ready to shed tears of happiness when the young lady kissed her and said she hoped they might be real friends. Daisy was now the household drudge, taking her mother's place. She had lost the bit of looks she once had; she was lean and scrawny, and her hair had lost its gloss and was seldom curled. But romance was still in her heart, nourished by the "pulps", and what could be more romantic than this runaway match of two young labor agitators just out of college? Somehow the fact that they were both "Reds" didn't count so heavily against them; Jim Bagg's wife had seen so much of workers' troubles through the depression years that she was ready to be told that a labor organizer was not what he was painted by the newspapers.

She had a topic of conversation with Dell; her little four-year-old who was rather peaked, and couldn't get much outdoor life in this winter weather. Dell knew all about vitamins and proteins and things, and told her what the little fellow ought to have, and how it could be got cheaply. That was Dell's job as a welfare worker, to ride here and there over the city and investigate the destitute and find out what they needed. She was tender-hearted and serious, and her heart bled for them because they could get so little of what they ought to have. It was a tough job, having anything to do with the poor nowadays, and the rich were well advised to put it off on salaried experts, college-trained.

Presently in came Abner, startled to be told he had a new daughter-in-law. He didn't know what to do or say, and was embarrassed when she came and kissed him on his leathery cheek, well streaked by greasy fingers. Abner couldn't have any idea what was in the soul of this young lady, so obviously refined in spite of being plainly dressed. He couldn't understand that she was disposed to idealize the working class, and to take his horny hand, the one finger gone and so many knobs and scars on the others, as symbols of honorable toil, the medals of a soldier of industry. But Abner could understand that she was a kind young lady, and that his son was lucky. That she sympathized with Tom's dangerous ideas did not surprise him. The old man had managed to develop water-tight compartments in his head, and could be sure that "agitators" were dangerous and wicked, and at the same time could talk with two of them and not disagree with anything they said.

## LXXXI

The movement to form industrial unions of the workers in big industry was spreading rapidly over the coun-

try; starting spontaneously in a thousand different places, born of the workers' desperate needs. All that had to be furnished was the policy and tactics; and these came from the big unions of the miners and the clothing workers, already organized by industries rather than by crafts. Presently there was formed the Committee for Industrial Organization, whose initials began to assume magical significance to millions of toilers who couldn't have told exactly what they stood for.

Money was put up by the big established unions, and organizers were sent to the different fields. So presently Tom Shutt had a job again. The fact that it paid only twenty-five dollars a week and ten dollars allowance for expenses was nothing against it in its holder's eyes; nor yet the fact that it was one of the most dangerous jobs in the world. In the city of Detroit a labor organizer was reasonably safe so long as he didn't go into dark corners alone; but in some of the smaller towns it was "open season" for trouble-makers—and this included the Ford towns, where Henry's billion dollars were taking care of themselves.

It was Tom's business to go into the neighborhood of the Ford plants, to meet the workers in their homes and elsewhere. He went; and before long a couple of plainclothes men stepped up to him and showed him their shields, and told him to come along. At police headquarters he sat confronting a captain of detectives and several of his aides. He told them his name and address, and his record: a graduate of the University of Michigan, a blacklisted Ford worker, and now an organizer of the United Automobile Workers of America. "I have a salary, and money in the bank, so you can't very well claim I have no visible means of support. I demand my right to telephone a lawyer, and I serve notice that if you deny the right, my first act on getting out will be to file suit for false arrest and imprisonment. What else do you want?"

"We want the names of the people you're working with."

"Well, you can lock me up and beat me till you break my guts, but you won't get a word about that. May I talk with my lawyer?"

"We'll give you a bit of a workout, young smartie," said the captain.

They took him into the basement, and put him in what they called "the hole", a dungeon with a small peephole in the steel door, and nothing inside but a stinking slop-pail and a water pail which had apparently been a slop-pail until recently. There he stayed, and every time he heard a footstep he wondered if they were coming with their rubber hoses.

The union kept a careful record of where its organizers were going, and required them to telephone the office every so often. When anyone failed to do so, it was assumed that the police had him. So now the word went out that Tom Shutt was missing, and the process of finding him began. The first stage was to telephone all the wives and mothers and sisters of the sympathizers and start them at work. The telephone at police headquarters would ring, and there would be an irate woman demanding to know about Tom Shutt. No denials were accepted, the police had him or knew where he was, and the speaker demanded his release. The sergeant would hang up the phone, and straight-

way it would ring again, and there would be another voice, making the same demand. Phone calls all day and all night, so that no police business could be transacted so long as Tom Shutt was held.

If a couple of hours of this didn't bring word from the prisoner, they would start on the company. It was a form of sabotage which might have been classified as "malicious mischief", but surely it wasn't any worse than holding a man in a dungeon without warrant or charge, and now and then beating him with rubber hoses which left no marks. A friend of the union would go to a drugstore or other place where there was a pay telephone, and call the administration building and ask for the president's office. A conversation would ensue:

"Is this the president's secretary?"

"Yes."

"I want Tom Shutt."

"Who is Tom Shutt?"

"He is an organizer of the United Automobile Workers of America. Your police have him in jail and we demand his release."

"We don't know anything about him."

"Report the matter to Mr. Edsel Ford, and tell him to get busy and find out about it. Your phone will be out of order until Tom Shutt is released."

Having said this, the caller would insert a tiny piece of match-stick under the lever supporting the telephone receiver. This kept the receiver from coming down all the way; and since the calling station controls the one called, the Ford Company's line would be "busy" until the telephone company sent a man to remedy the trouble. Meantime the caller had moved on to the next pay station and repeated the performance. It cost only five cents a shot, and with several men on the job, all the trunk lines into the Ford administration building would soon be reporting "busy", and high-salaried executives trying to get New York or Chicago to conclude million-dollar contracts would have to hop into their cars and drive somewhere else to place the calls. "Tom Shutt? Who is Tom Shutt?" everybody in the place would be asking, and thousands of white-collar workers would whisper: "It's the union! They're trying to get a union at Ford's!"

## LXXXII

Tom Shutt came out. But there was another prisoner in a dungeon who stayed, with no hope of release. That was the Flivver King, the prisoner of a billion dollars; there were chains upon his legs, making certain that he would never walk alone, and chains upon his mind, so that he would think no thought of which the billion dollars did not approve. These dollars told him that he was the object of deadly mass hatred; that half a million people blamed him for having sentenced them to slow starvation; that there was a nation-wide, indeed a world-wide conspiracy to take his fortune from him. The farm-boy who had been gay and talkative had turned morose and bitter, and stayed by himself for the most part, watching his guards to make sure that they watched him.

Henry Ford, who had once been the best of employers, had become the worst. His rivals had passed him, and

he was paying the lowest wages in the industry; his workers were getting an average of less than a thousand dollars a year. His speed-up was the most ruthless, his shop was a by-word among the workers. Sixteen years previously he had stated publicly that the men might have unions if they wanted them; now he said, secretly, that any man who mentioned the subject would be immediately fired, and to make that good he had more kinds of spies than had ever before been known in the United States of America.

All Henry's thinking was dominated by a grim historical precedent. There had been another ruler who owned a billion dollars, the Tsar of all the Russias. In the year 1905 his dissatisfied workers had come to his palace demanding a hearing, and had been shot down by machine-guns. Some thirteen years later that Tsar and his wife and lovely daughters had been shot in a cellar. The Flivver King had done the same thing to his workers, and under the same circumstances. Of course he hadn't done it personally, any more than poor Nicky had; in each case it was the billion dollars which had committed the crime—but alas, it was not the billion dollars which had been shot in the cellar.

I am greatness, I am power, I am pride, pomp, and dominion, said the fortune of Henry Ford; I am a dynasty, surviving into the distant future, making history which will not be "bunk", carrying the name of Ford and the glory of Ford to billions of unborn people. But there are evil men, devils in human form loose in the world, who plot to take that glory from me; who desire that the world shall talk, not about Henry and Edsel, and Henry II, and Benson, and Josephine Clay, and William Ford, now fully grown and ready for their share of glory, but about persons with names such as Trotsky and Zinoviev and Bela Kun and Radek and Liebknecht and Luxemburg and Jaurès and Blum.

Henry thought of Jewish names, for the reason that his recantation on the subject of the Jews had been purely a business move, and he was just as convinced as ever that the great conspiracy against his billion dollars was that Jewish-Bolshevik conspiracy which had been exposed in the "Dearborn Independent." In statement after statement Henry charged that the movement for industrial organization of the workers was a Communist plot, and that it was secretly financed by banking interests which desired to break the Ford Motor Company and turn it over to Wall Street. To add that these Communist leaders and big bankers were international Jews was a detail which said itself. The man who had been editor of the "Dearborn Independent" and had written the anti-Jewish articles was now Henry's confidential secretary, the publicity man who controlled all his contacts with the outside world. William J. Cameron hadn't changed his views a particle, but on the contrary was in contact with anti-Semitic agencies all over the world, and kept Henry in contact with them.

## LXXXIII

"What shall I do?" asked the Flivver King; and the billion dollars was at his ear, whispering like Mephistopheles into the ear of Faust:

"Look, Mr. Ford, it's already been done. The Reds seized the factories in Italy, but now a strong man has made that country safe for business. Look at Germany. No Reds agitating to seize the automobile factories in that country! The way of salvation is clear; but you have to act quickly, put these rats down before their power grows too great. Learn from us; let us do the job!"

The billion dollars surrounded its captive with Nazi agents and Fascist whisperers. They had begun upon him early, when Hitler's movement was young; they had got forty thousand dollars from him to reprint the anti-Jewish pamphlets in German translations, the names of Hitler and Ford appearing jointly in the advertising. Later on a grandson of the ex-Kaiser had come to Ford's and got a job, and had been the agent through whom three hundred thousand dollars had been forwarded to the Nazi party treasury. Henry had big factories in Germany, and it was no utopian idealism for him to have strikes prevented in that country.

Now came Fritz Kuhn, Hitler's number one organizer in America, uniformed head of the marching and drilling German-American Bund. He moved his headquarters to Detroit and took a job as one of Henry's chemists. A new anti-Semitic campaign was started, and the Nazis swarmed at Ford's; grim, determined men who shared with Henry the characteristic which had made his fortune, that when they wanted something they wanted it at once, and took the necessary steps to get it. They were now doing their work in every country of the world;

they had murdered the Roumanian premier and the Austrian chancellor, the King of Jugoslavia and a minister of France; they had kidnapped and killed hundreds of their political opponents in Central Europe, and even in France. Now into the ears of the aged Flivver King they whispered:

"Here is what you need, Mr. Ford: a pure, native, hundred percent American movement, combining all the others —the Ku Klux Klan, the Black Legion, the Silver Shirts, the Crusader Whiteshirts, the American Liberty League, the Anglo-Saxon Federation— all movements pledged to put down the Reds and preserve the property interests of the country; to oust the Bolshevik from the White House and all his pink professors from the government services; to put all the foreign agitators on ships of stone with sails of lead and start them out to sea; to make it a shooting offense to talk Communism or to call a strike.

"All that is needed is money, Mr. Ford; money for silver shirts and black hoods, money for boots to march in and for flags to wave; for brass knucks and revolvers and machine-guns and armored cars and gas-bombs; for propaganda leaflets, anti-Jewish newspapers, Brown Houses and Ford radio hours. Anyone who has money nowadays can make the people believe anything; and if you give us enough, we will build a political party and elect one of our agents President of the United States. Give us one percent of your fortune, Mr. Ford, and we will make America safe for the other ninety-nine percent!"

Henry listened and found this good. For Henry remained what he had been born; a supermechanic with the mind of a stubborn peasant.

## LXXXIV

Towards sundown of a warm spring evening the Flivver King strolled about the garden of his farm, looking at his birds. It was here that he had provided two thousand bird-houses, warmed by electricity in winter, and with a water-supply protected against freezing. Here he had turned loose three hundred and eighty pairs of English song-birds, and at another time seventy-five pairs of martens. He was interested to see how many could be tempted to remain over the winter in these luxurious quarters, and how many returned each spring. He counted them, and the figures interested him almost as much as the daily sales and production reports of his cars.

At the same hour Tom Shutt met his wife in one of those proletarian joints where you get sinkers and coffee, or maybe "ham and", and put the tray on the wide arm of a chair. Tom was scheduled to speak at a meeting, and Dell, who was brave outside but terrified within, would never let him go alone. She came to meet him as soon as her work was finished, and thereafter stuck by his side. "I can always scream," she said.

At seven o'clock Henry's man came and reminded him that he had to dress. The Flivver King came into the house grumbling, because he hated formal affairs; his wife had to make the dates and hold him to them. This was a special occasion, a dinner-party at the home of one of those old families who had had dignity and possessions in Detroit when Henry Ford was a farmboy learning to take a watch apart. Now he was a hundred times as rich as they could hope to be, but he still

looked upon them with secret awe, and
had yielded to their plea to show them
the good old-time fun which he was laboring to revive in America.

At that hour Tom and Dell were
finishing their twenty-five cent supper,
and Dell was looking anxiously for
two friends who had promised to join
them. Tom's car was only a "coop",
and the wife always tried to get some
other car to follow them to meetings.
She didn't talk about it much, because
she didn't want to weaken her husband's nerve, but she thought continually about the organizer who had been
murdered less than a year back, and the
other who had been shot a while before
that.

At seven-thirty Henry and his wife
stepped into their limousine. It was
fortunate he had bought the Lincoln
company, and so had a suitable car of
his own to ride in. The chauffeur put
a robe over their knees and they settled
back for a drive to the fashionable
Grosse Pointe district. "I counted
seven linnets," said Henry. "I wonder
if they are descendants of that pair
which nested over our front door.
How long ago was that? Twenty-
two years—my, how time flies! It
would be interesting to know how long
a linnet lives. I will band some of
the young ones this season."

At that time Tom and his wife, followed by a second car with friends in
it, had reached the neighborhood of
the meeting, and parked their cars and
locked them. The hall was on the second floor, over a feed-store; there was
a street-light immediately in front of
it, and therefore few people were in
sight. In back was an entrance by an
outside stairway, and there a file of
men and women with handkerchiefs

over their faces were mounting the
stairs and groping their way in darkness to empty seats. Nearly all were
Ford workers; some of them the same
of whom Henry had stated sixteen
years ago that they could have unions
if they wanted them.

## LXXXV

Henry Ford prided himself upon being always on time. At precisely eight
o'clock he and his wife descended from
their limousine under the brightly
lighted porte-cochere of a mansion; not
such an elaborate mansion, according
to the standards of the motor-kings and
money-kings of the Detroit area, but
having the advantage that it was nearly
sixty years old. A footman in decor-
ous black took their wraps, and escorted them into a drawing-room with
old furniture which warmed the heart
of the collector. They were greeted
by the elderly host and hostess, and
their son and daughter-in-law, all quiet
and gracious people. The farmboy
was impressed.

At this same hour the chairman of
the meeting was telling the audience
that no liberties had ever been won in
this world without a struggle. Such
rights as Americans now enjoyed were
theirs because men had been willing to
fight and die for them. It would be
the same with their rights as workers;
industrial feudalism would not give up
without a struggle, and without heroes
to make sacrifices for the cause.

At eight-fifteen the guests were
served with cocktails, some made with
Bacardi and some with tomato juice.
Henry and his wife took the latter.
They had a wide choice of hors d'oeuvres
made of pâté de foie gras smeared upon

little crackers, and caviar on diamond-shaped pieces of toast, and anchovies on rye bread, and bits of ham and tiny sausages on skewers—in short so many fancy things that your eye did not have time to take them all in or your mind to identify them. They were salty, and awakened anticipations.

The chairman was introducing the speaker of the evening, a blacklisted Ford worker. The chairman would have liked to add that he was the son of a Ford worker, but Tom had asked him not to mention that. He said that the speaker came from a family of factory workers, his father and grandfather before him had shared the troubles which now the workers of the Detroit area were determined to end.

At close to eight-thirty the sixteen guests were seated in the dining-room, where oil-painted ancestors looked down upon a scene of quiet elegance. The table had an open-work cloth, like heavy lace, through which shone polished mahogany. Hothouse roses were strewn upon it, lovely in the light of tall candles in silver holders. There was old-fashioned hand-cut glass, and family monogram silver, the pieces carefully laid in the proper order. In short, a meal served according to tradition, by a hostess who had known from childhood how it should be done, and had trained her servants so that everything moved like one of Henry's perfect machines.

Tom Shutt was telling his unseen audience the elementary facts about the condition of the working class under competitive capitalism. They confronted enormous aggregations of capital—big business, said Tom, endeavoring to correct his collegiate tendency to use big words. Alone and by themselves the workers were helpless. The masses of unemployed would bid them down, bit by bit, until we would have in America standards like those of the coolies in China; they would hustle at their work like rickshawmen, and be old and done for at forty. Only one way to avoid that fate—to unite, and confront the boss with a monopoly equal to his own.

## LXXXVI

The hostess who had planned the dinner-party had faced something of a problem. She knew that her distinguished guest was a plain American, after the fashion of her own grandfather long since departed. She doubted if he would appreciate the arts of her chef, and was sure he would not know how to pronounce the names of French foods. Since they were to dance old-fashioned American dances, the occasion seemed to call for old-fashioned American food. But how could one serve such food without appearing—well, a bit obvious? She had asked a venerable uncle what their forefathers had eaten for salad, and his answer had been, "Turnip-tops, and we drank the pot-likker." But she hadn't the nerve for that, and comforted herself with the thought that alligator pears grow in Florida. There was no need to bring up the question, for Mr. Ford, in the seat of honor at her right hand, talked about his English birds while he ate his salad.

Tom Shutt explained to his unseen audience the stage to which big business had come. The automobile industry had the plant capacity to produce twice the number of cars which the American people had money to buy.

The three big fellows were competing so fiercely that they didn't dare start production until the last moment, each afraid that his spies might overlook some new improvement and let the other fellow get ahead of him. So the year's work was jammed into two or three months; the men were driven like race-horses during that period, and the rest of the time were turned out to live on the breadlines.

The second course was a terrapin-soup, and the hostess felt safe in making allusion to this, because her forefathers had come from the "Eastern shore", and she was in position to establish the early American credentials of the diamond-back terrapin. The compliments upon the delicious flavor of her offering ran round the table, and reached the ears of the distinguished guest, causing him to forget the warnings of his physician on the subject of big dinner-parties.

Tom Shutt couldn't see any member of his audience, but he could hear them, and they were not slow in letting him know what they thought about his arguments. Were they getting a living wage out of the motor industry? Were they able to buy the products of the factories and the farms? They made plain that they were not; and Tom told them that their troubles could be summed up in one simple statement: that under the New Deal profits had increased fifty percent while wages had increased only ten percent. So the very factor which had caused the depression was working faster than ever, leading them straight to another smashup, unless they could find a way to increase wages at the expense of profits.

The next course was a quail. There could be no doubt that our forefathers had had these in abundance; although they had not been able to serve them in little casseroles of fire-resistant glass, and it was to be doubted if they had known how to prepare such a delicious mushroom sauce. These warm-hearted little creatures, flying so fast and far, have need of bulging breast-muscles, each side of which makes a couple of delicious bites for a diner; but you would be well advised not to try to eat any more of them at such an elegant function as this, where you had to wipe your fingers on delicate hand-embroidered napkins.

The orator was dealing with the problem of how to increase wages. Politics was a tricky art, he said, and the Chief Justice of the United States Supreme Court was our authority for the statement that the laws are what the judges say they are. But the power of the workers organized into one union was a thing which no legal tricks could thwart. A billion-dollar industrial empire such as Ford's could be met and matched by only one thing, a union of the two hundred thousand Ford workers, controlled by the democratic will of its membership. That was what they meant to have, because it was the only way out of misery and despair for the producing masses.

## LXXXVII

The hostess was creating a bit of a sensation with flat molds of ice cream, each an exact imitation of the new streamlined Ford, the Victory-8 model which had swept the country and gone into million car production. With it came little round cakes of a dark color, perfect reproductions of automobile wheels, the spokes made of thin threads of hard sugar, inserted into the hubs and rims. The laughter and discussion pleased the great manufacturer, who was used to all sorts of Ford jokes, and took them all as advertising.

Could the old-line labor unions do this job? Tom Shutt was asking. Could they do it, even if they had honest leaders, interested in the unskilled or semi-skilled workers of the mass industries? They could not do it, because the very basis of their organization was wrong. The old-style craft unions had been made for the days of small enterprises; to use them today was like taking a horse and buggy out upon a modern high speed motorway. Imagine Ford's with a hundred different unions, all fighting for jurisdiction; dividing up the River Rouge plant among carpenters, machinists, steamfitters, glass-workers, truck-drivers! All these workers now had one boss, and let that boss deal with one union.

The velvet-footed servitors were bringing coffee in delicate little china cups which had come from England in the early days, and were guarded as family heirlooms, washed under the eye of the housekeeper, at a distance from water-faucets. This led to interesting conversation with Mr. Ford, who knew a lot about china, and said he would like to buy this set for his museum, if ever the day came that the lady could bring herself to part with it. Swiftly in her secret soul the lady weighed the value of these heirlooms against the power of the Ford banks, and the possibility of a family alliance with one of the Ford grandchildren; then with a sudden burst of generosity she presented the treasures to her guest. Henry with a burst of gratitude told his wife about it, and as she was seated

at the other end of the table, this also was a form of advertising, a fair return for V-8 ice cream.

"Organize!" Tom Shutt was crying, pounding the speaker's table at risk of upsetting the water pitcher in the dark. "Make up your minds that you are going to demand and win your full share of the products of high-speed machinery. Fix firmly in mind this basic idea, that America today has the means of producing an abundance of everything for everybody—food, clothing, shelter, health, education, recreation. Decent homes for the workers do not exist, but they can be built in a short time; there is no excuse in America for poverty for those who are willing to work. Demand your share! Keep on demanding, over and over, until the just demand is granted!"

It was half-past nine and the guests had moved into the drawing-room, where they chatted about the state of the market and the money situation, meanwhile being served liqueurs in tiny glasses. Mrs. Ford was telling the daughter-in-law about their English song-birds, which this young lady had studied in their native haunts. Mr. Ford was being shown a Sheraton table, inlaid with the portrait of some English nobleman. He graciously offered to send one of his experts to fix the date of the table and identify the portrait.

Tom's meeting was over, and since it had begun to rain quite hard, some of the people were running to their cars, and others waiting, crowded into the doorways. Several men who had been hanging around outside were pushing here and there, peering into the faces of the workers. Everyone knew what that meant, and those who didn't want to be recognized pulled their coats over their heads and made off in spite of the rain. Others let themselves be jostled, because there was no good getting into a fight with company thugs who were always armed and ready for trouble.

## LXXXVIII

The guests were taken to the ballroom, which comprised the top floor of the mansion, and had recently been done over in cream and gold, with heavy crimson curtains between the tall windows. Gilt Louis Quinze chairs lined the walls, and here sat other guests who had been invited for the dancing. There was a raised dais for the musicians—no jazz-band, but three fiddlers, skinny old men with whiskers, the only persons in the company who did not wear evening dress. They grinned happily, revealing the fact that one had store teeth, and another had only a few, and the third had only two—"but thank God they hits," said he.

Tom and Dell hurried to their car, their friends behind them, running in the rain. The cars started, and then began to slow up—bump, bump. Tom's car had a "flat", something that can happen when you are trying to save money and are driving on the fabric. They stopped, and Tom hopped out and went to work, one of his friends helping—not such fun in a rainstorm. But they would soon be home and get out of their wet clothes. The young fellows made a joke of it, while Dell watched anxiously.

The fiddlers struck up: Turkey in the Straw, jolly old jig-tune to which millions of pioneers danced on festival occasions. To let your mind dwell on these ancestors was a heart-warming thing, giving you a sense of the mass of life which lay behind you, the high deeds, the traditions to which you were heir. The old fiddler with the longest whiskers and the store teeth called the numbers. "Grand march. All form". The couples lined up and paraded round the hall, gay and playful, but proud, too, knowing themselves the most important people in this part of the world; perfectly nurtured, perfectly groomed, the ladies with shining bosoms and arms, clad in silks and satins and filmy fabrics of bright hues, the gentlemen vigorous and capable, now in a mood of gallantry, some of the younger ones in white coats, quite decorative. All marching, laughing to one another, and to the fiddlers as they passed. A charming scene—yes, these old dances were a pleasant novelty.

Tom had got his spare on, and they were turning into a great boulevard, followed by the car of their friends; Dell looking out behind, trying to see if there was any other car, but finding it hard to see in the rain. They talked about the meeting, the behavior of the crowd, the contents of the weekly paper which the union was publishing and which had been given away free at the door. There were many things to do and to think about; the harvest plenteous and the laborers few.

## LXXXIX

It was half-past ten o'clock, and the guests were dancing a Lancers; four sets, thirty-two people, nearly everyone present. "Old Zip Coon" was the tune, and the three fiddlers were sawing away, one of them calling as he had called in a backwoods village in his youth, when corn-huskings and cabin-raisings were occasions for festivities. "Honor your partners"—the gentlemen bowed to their ladies. "Lady on the left"—they bowed to the next gentleman's partner. "All join hands and circle to the left"—the gentleman gave his left hand to the lady on his left and turned her, and then taking his partner's right hand proceeded round the circle, right hand, left hand, ladies coming towards you. Not all these people knew the old dances, and they had fun setting one another straight.

Tom and Dell had come to the place where their friends were due to turn off. The friends offered to follow them all the way home, but Tom said no, they were all right, it wasn't far; Tom was easy-going, sure of himself, and Dell didn't like to worry him with continual suggestions of fear. There was nobody following them, apparently. "Well, good night, fine meeting, good speech you made, see you in the morning, so long"—calling to one another from the cars.

The old prompter was turning loose, spreading his feathers, showing his style; calling the numbers in singsong, and adding verses: "Right hand grand around the ring; hand over hand with the dear little thing." Homely comments and instruction: "Left allemande, right hand grand, plant your taters in a sandy land." All very gay, everybody falling into the spirit of the occasion, stomping their feet—it was as Henry had said, you couldn't dance these old dances without coming into contact with many people, having your heart warmed to them, being moved to kindness and fellowship. They were a civilizing force.

Tom and his wife had turned off the main boulevard, passing from the outskirts of one town to those of another. Open fields, some warehouses, railroad tracks to be crossed carefully on a rainy night. Tom was telling about a committee meeting in headquarters and disagreements over tactics; Dell wasn't listening very closely, looking behind her, trying to see out of the little rear window with the rain streaming down.

## XC

The moment had come for which the guests had been waiting, the big treat which had been promised. Four chosen couples were to dance a quadrille; four elderly couples, dignified and distinguished, to show the younger people how much there really was in these old square-dances. Mrs. Ford had for her partner the leading banker of Detroit, and Henry's partner was this banker's wife. The prompter on his dignity, no more fooling. "First four right and left," he called; the tune was "The Girl I Left Behind Me." Henry, grey-haired, and spare as he had always been, took the hand of his stately lady, and moved seriously yet smiling through the measures. It had been a minuet which the old kings and emperors danced, but the Flivver King was an American, and the American way was best. When the old fiddler from the backwoods of Michigan called "Promenade," it rhymed with "lemonade"—the proper drink to serve at parties.

Behind Tom and Dell a car came speeding. There was a sudden squealing of brakes, and the car swung in, its wheels just missing Tom's, and forcing him to the curb. "Hey, what the hell?" Dell's heart gave an agonized leap; she knew what it was—the hideous thing of which she had been living in terror. They were helpless, unarmed—for a labor organizer may not carry arms, he counts himself lucky if the police do not plant a gun on him and send him up for a year or two.

"Ladies' chain," called the prompter; and Mrs. Ford, in lovely pale blue chiffon, gave her right hand to the lady at her left, and they crossed to the opposite gentlemen, to give their left hands, and be turned, and come back to their partners. The gentleman opposite to Mrs. Ford was her beloved husband, and she beamed upon him, and squeezed his hand as she took it. The best of men, and the wisest—had he not rediscovered this charming form of diversion, and made it known to this gracious company? Such power for good he had.

Five men leaped from the car and rushed upon the "coop" of the Shutts. Tom sprang out; he was not going to give up without a fight. Dell had promised to scream, and did so; she got out of the car to scream louder, but one of the men threw himself upon her and bowled her over. She bit his hand as he tried to hold her mouth; he rolled her over and jammed her face into the mud, so that instead of screaming she began to choke and presently was lying still. Tom got in a couple of hearty blows, just enough to get his assailants worked up; then one of them landed him a kick in the groin, and he went down with the four on top of him.

"Promenade," called the prompter, and then, "All balance partners."

Henry's usually pale face was flushed with happiness and pride. The stoutish but elegant lady in green silk who was his partner smiled upon him, the diamond sunburst upon her corsage dazzled his eyes, and he knew that this was a grand world which he had helped to make, and that no one stood higher in it than himself.

Two of the men had dragged Tom's hands behind his back and slipped handcuffs upon them. The other two drew blackjacks from under their coats, leather clubs with lead in the ends, and proceeded to work on him —not his head, which might spoil his enjoyment of the process, but beating every inch of his body systematically, so that it would be black and blue.

"Right and left hand promenade," called the prompter. Two couples crossed to one another's places; the partners took hands crossed, and walked back to their places, passing the other couple to the right, and when they had reached their places, the gentleman, still holding the lady's hand, turned her into her place.

The gangsters were making a professional job of it. They had Tom on his side and were kicking him in the small of his back to loosen his kidneys.

"Chassez out", called the prompter; the old-timers always pronounced it "Shashay." And then, "Form lines." The dancers moved with perfect grace, knowing every move.

The chief executioner was now kicking his victim in the groin, so that he would not be of much use to his wife for a while.

"Six hands around the ladies," called the prompter. Such charming smiles from elderly ladies, playing at coquetry, renewing their youth.

"Okey," said the leader. One of them stooped and unlocked the handcuffs and put them in his pocket. They called to the fifth man, who still had his knee in Dell's back, having considerately turned her head sideways so that she would not suffocate.

"All forward and back," called the prompter. They tripped lightly with little half-steps.

The five men jumped into their car and sped swiftly away.

### XCI

The quadrille was over, and the hostess came to Henry to thank him. Others gathered about. "Really charming, Mr. Ford. . . . Most enjoyable. . . . A delightful occasion. . . . You have conferred a boon upon us." Henry beamed; for these were people who counted, what they said had weight. His crusade was a success. People laughed at him—many times they had laughed at him, but in the end they always had to acknowledge that he was right.

Dell Shutt was crawling feebly in the mud; she kept moaning, "Tom! Tom!" The beating of the rain on the ground drowned her voice. She was in an agony of terror, so that she did not feel her bodily pain. Was he dead? Had they carried him away? "Tom! Where are you?" She fainted again.

Henry and his wife were taking their departure; he never kept late hours. Those who liked to dance half the night would stay; they would turn on the radio and have jazz music—his victory was not complete, but this wouldn't be mentioned to him. People came to shake hands and thank him

again. He was the most important of men, and it was worth while to keep one's self in his mind. He placed enormous contracts, kept huge deposits in the banks, ruled the destinies of an empire. Also, his wife was a social leader—and little personal touches count with women. "So glad to have seen you again—and looking so well. . . . Drop in on us some day. . . . Don't forget next Friday. . . . Your dancing is delightful, Mrs. Ford."

Dell had come to her senses again. Her head was ringing, her teeth chattering, her hands and feet were like ice. She began crawling again, and calling, "Tom!" Her voice wouldn't come, there seemed to be mud in her throat and she couldn't get it out.

The Fords were donning their wraps. "The nights stay chilly," said the host, who accompanied them to the door. "I can't tell you what pleasure you have given us." The chauffeur held the door of the limousine open, and placed warm robes over their knees. The guard who rode by the chauffeur's side stood at the other side of the car. He never did anything but watch; his gun in an open holster, decorously covered by a flap of his coat. Behind them was a second fast car, with two armed guards in it, and these stood facing in different directions, doing nothing but watch. Gangsters were active these days, and stopped at nothing.

Dell had come upon the body of her husband, still unconscious. She started screaming and sobbing, but soon realized that that wouldn't help. He felt cold, but not so cold as the rain and the mud. His face was upturned and his mouth open; she managed to turn him onto his side, fearing that he might choke and be drowned. She could see by the lights where the boulevard was, and desperation gave her strength; she got to her feet and staggered towards it.

## XCII

"Don't be cynical, Henry," Mrs. Ford was saying, as their car sped towards home.

"What's the good fooling yourself about people?" asked Henry. "They all have something to sell."

"Most of those people have all the money they need, I am sure."

"All the same, there's not one of them but wants more, and would be glad to get it out of you or me. The first step is to get to know you."

"Such thoughts poison human relationships, dear."

"Well, I never took the trouble to put on glad rags and go out unless I was after something, and my guess is it's the same with them."

"The dancing was beautiful."

"It was all right. But I'll bet they're dancing jazz right now."

The chauffeur and the guard were cut off from this conversation by a glass partition in the car. They kept their eyes fixed on the road ahead. Passing a stretch of vacant land, they saw through the rain a woman coming towards the road   She appeared to be staggering, and as they came near she began waving, and running faster, as if to intercept them, they had to swerve to avoid her. The second car, close behind, swerved also.

"What was that?" asked the chauffeur.

"Maybe she's drunk," said the guard.

The car sped on. They had their orders, they stopped for nothing. They were carrying a billion dollars, and such a sum of money cannot manifest either sympathy or curiosity; it has enough to do to take care of itself.

Henry and his wife had not observed the episode. They were settled back in their seats, resting. They were not so young as they had been.

"You should let yourself be happier, dear," the wife was saying. "You have done a great deal of good in the world."

"Have I?" said the Flivver King. "Sometimes I wonder, can anybody do any good. If anybody knows where this world is heading, he knows a lot more than me."

# OTHER BOOKS *from* CHARLES H. KERR

**JOE HILL: The IWW & the Making of a Revolutionary Workingclass Count erculture**, by Franklin Rosemont. A new in-depth study of the famous Wobbly bard, and of the IWW counterculture he came to personify. Discusses in detail Hill's views on capitalism, race/gender issues, religion, and wilderness, as well as songwriting. Several chapters explore his little-known work as cartoonist. *"Joe Hill has finally found a chronicler worthy of his revolutionary spirit, sense of humor, and poetic imagination"*—**Robin D. G. Kelley**. *"The best book ever written on Joe Hill"*—**Utah Phillips**. 656 pages. Illustrated. Cloth $35. Paper $19.

**LABOR STRUGGLES IN THE DEEP SOUTH & Other Writings** by Covington Hall. Edited and Introduced by David R. Roediger. Published for the first time this book formerly only found in Rare book libraries, is an underground classic work of organizing among the timber and dock workers in Louisiana and East Texas in the 1910s. 262p. $14.00

**A HISTORY OF PAN-AFRICAN REVOLT** by C. L. R. James, with an Introduction by Robin D. G. Kelley. The classic account of global Black resistance in Africa and the diaspora. *"A mine of ideas advancing far ahead of its time"* —Walter Rodney. 160 pages. $12.00

**CRIME AND CRIMINALS & OTHER WRITINGS** by Clarence Darrow, with an essay by Leon Despres and an Afterword by Carol Heise. The great labor attorney's "Address to the Prisoners in the Cook County Jail" and other hardhit-ting indictments of the U.S. Criminal justice system. *"First and last, people are sent to jail because they are poor"*—Darrow. 64 pages, Illustrated. $7.50

**FELLOW WORKER: The Life of Fred Thompson**, compiled and introduced by Dave Roediger. The fascinating and highly informative memoirs of an old-time Wobbly, socialist, organizer, soapboxer, class-war prisoner, educator, editor, historian and publisher. 94 pages. Illustrated. $10.00

**FROM BUGHOUSE SQUARE TO THE BEAT GENERATION: Selected Ravings of Slim Brundage**, Founder/Janitor of the College of Complexes. Edited/Introduced by Franklin Rosemont. An old Wobbly relates his life in the 1920s IWW/Bughouse Square counterculture to the Beat Generation and New Left of the 1950s and 60s. 176 pp. Illustrated. $14.00

**THE COMMUNIST MANIFESTO** by Karl Marx & Frederick Engels.150th Anniversary Edition of the revolutionary classic that has been continuously in print from Charles H. Kerr since 1902. This handsome new edition features an important critical Introduction by Robin D. G. Kelley. 64 pages. $5.00

**THE STORY OF MARY MACLANE & OTHER WRITINGS** by Mary MacLane, edited & introduced by Penelope Rosemont. Memoir of a rebellious Montana 19-year-old; the publishing scandal of 1902, its freshness and audacity haven't aged a bit. With reviews of the book by Henry Blake Fuller, Clarence Darrow, and Harriet Monroe. 218 pages. Illustrated. $15.00

**ISADORA SPEAKS: Writings & Speeches of Isadora Duncan**, edited & introduced by Franklin Rosemont, with a preface by Ann Barzel. Expanded edition, with many new illustrations. *"A tremendously provocative and inform-ative book"*—Agnes DeMille. 176 pages. Profusely illus. $12.00

*Please add $2.50 postage for the first title, and fifty cents for each additional title.*

## CHARLES H. KERR PUBLISHING COMPANY
1726 West Jarvis Avenue, Chicago, IL 60626/charleshkerr.net

CPSIA information can be obtained at www.ICGtesting.com
Printed in the USA
LVOW04s1740070115

421885LV00017B/996/P

9 780882 863573